Rori

By

Ronna M. Bacon

Copyright © 2024 Ronna M. Bacon
ISBN 978-1-998821-57-0

Isaiah 40:10. Fear not, for I am with you; be not dismayed, for I am your God; I will strengthen you, I will help you, I will uphold you with my righteous right hand. NKJV

Table of Contents

Chapter 1
Chapter 2
Chapter 3
Chapter 4
Chapter 5
Chapter 6
Chapter 7
Chapter 8
Chapter 9
Chapter 10
Chapter 11
Chapter 12
Chapter 13
Chapter 14
Chapter 15
Chapter 16
Chapter 17
Chapter 18
Chapter 19
Chapter 20
Chapter 21
Chapter 22
Chapter 23
Chapter 24
Chapter 25
Chapter 26
Chapter 27
Chapter 28
Chapter 29
Chapter 30
Chapter 31

Chapter 32
Chapter 33
Chapter 34
Chapter 35
Chapter 36
Chapter 37
Chapter 38
Chapter 39
Chapter 40
Chapter 41
Epilogue
Dear Readers

Chapter 1

Shoving himself upright to rest his hand against the damp earth, Rori Reade hung his head down. His arm was shaking almost too much to hold him upright. His other arm came up to wipe across his face before he looked up. That arm helped to shade the sun glaring down at him. Rori frowned. He had no idea where he was or even how he got there. His gaze dropped as unfocused as it was as he glanced around. Rori only saw dirt around him. That he could not understand.

His arm collapsed, sending Rori back to the dirt under him and back into oblivion. His deep brown eyes closed as he lost consciousness, his dark blond curls covered in debris. Rori, even if conscious, could not have said how he ended up in a hole in the ground, a hole too deep for him to climb out of.

Hours seemed to pass with Rori rousing slightly and then dropping back into that well. He didn't hear the rustle about him of the forest critters moving about their daily walk. The sun traced its path through the sky until late afternoon.

Sounds of heavy footfalls sounded through the forest, disturbing the critters who ran for cover, peeking out at the two men who stomped towards the trap that they had set. They had not planned on catching a human being but rather some sort of wild animal.

The younger of the two men, rough in clothing and mannerisms, peered down into the hole, shock on his face. His whiskered and unkempt face turned towards the older man.

"Pa? Who's that? That's not what we wanted." His voice was slurred from the alcohol and drugs that were his mainstay in life.

"Whadda ya mean?" The older man, just as unkempt and dirty in appearance, peered down as well. "Who's that?"

"I dunno." The younger man looked around, seeming to feel watched. He shrugged before he looked back down into the hole. "Whadda we do with him?"

His father shrugged.

"Leave him. We'll just dig another hole and try again." He walked away, his gait as unsteady as his son's who followed closely behind him.

"But Pa? What can we do with him? Can we sell him to someone?" The younger man ducked the blow aimed at his head, years of experience helping to avoid being swatted.

"No, we ain't doing that. We leave him. No one will miss him."

The men disappeared from sight, not hearing the whistle and singing from the three younger people heading their way on another path. The older of the three, a young lady around Rori's age, paused for a moment, sensing danger to some extent before she moved forward, the younger man and lady walking ahead of her by a few paces. Laughter sprinkled through the air, the three not realizing the danger that hovered in the forest around them. They didn't see the man standing near the hole in the ground, his gaze shifting between that and the path the three were on.

"Brit?" The younger of the two, a young lady, turned to her sister. "Something's wrong. What is it?"

Brit Morrison paused for a moment, her eyes searching the area. She shivered with fear, somehow sensing that when they stepped from the path that they were walking, things would change for her. Her violet eyes were troubled and shadowed, not just from that day but from what she had been facing over the last few months. She tugged at her red gold braid for a moment, watching her younger brother and sister as they walked ahead of her. Brit was worried about them, not sure as to why, but knowing that they were facing something that she really didn't want to face.

Brit's brother, Bevan, turned to watch his sister. His colouring was similar to hers and their sister, Becc. He felt a sudden sense of dread for her, his eyes searching as well. Brit had raised them since their mother passed away when Brit was about twenty-one and the two younger than her by six and seven years. Their father had walked out on his family when the two younger were not even into their teens. The bond between the siblings was closer than normal just because of that.

Bevan's arm suddenly was thrown out, stopping Becc in her tracks and causing Brit to stop as well.

"Bevan? Why did you do that?" Becc's voice sounded loud in the sudden silence.

"Because of that!" Bevan pointed towards the hole in the ground. "That wasn't there last week when we walked through here."

Brit moved around her brother, heading for the hole and then staring at it. She frowned, hearing a soft sound from down in it. Her hand reached for her brother's before she leaned over, studying the depth of the hole and then drawing in a sharp breath.

"There's someone down there, guys. We need to get down there." She looked around. "It's not that deep, not really. But I think he's hurt." She spun to face the two. "Becc, the rope that you insisted that we needed today?"

Becc was nodding, already shrugging out of her backpack and reaching inside it.

"God told me to bring it, Brit. He really and truly did." The three were strong believers and fully trusted that God would direct them that way.

"Brit? Who's going down?" Bevan was already tying off the rope to a tree before he stood in front of his sister.

"I am. Here." She dropped her backpack and then reached for her phone. "We have service. Call it in, Becc. Bevan, help me."

Brit was over the side of the hole, her hands almost sliding down the rope. She paused as her feet hit the debris on the bottom of the pit, staring up at her brother for a moment before she was on her knees, her hands reaching to assess the young man.

Sitting back in shock, Brit stared at Rori. They were acquainted from church activities although she could not say that they were friends. How did he get down here, she wondered? And for how long?

"Rori?" Her voice was low as she tried to rouse him to no avail. She looked up as Becc leaned over.

"Brit? They're on their way. They want to know how he is."

"He's unconscious, Becc. I don't know how hurt he is or how long he's been here. I want to know who dug this hole and why." Brit's hand rested against Rori's cheek, finding his head turning into her hand. She frowned for a moment, not having expected that. "Rori?" Her voice was low.

Rori's eyes flickered open for a moment before they closed. He just wasn't able to stay alert even hearing the soft and melodious female voice calling his name. He sighed and then groaned as he moved, hurting in ways that he didn't think that he could hurt.

Chapter 2

Brit quickly scaled back up from the bottom of the hole, Bevan reaching to help her steady herself once more on the surface even as Becc moved in to hug her. She turned to watch as the emergency services personnel moved in, one of the paramedic quickly disappearing towards Rori. She moved back from the hole as she was requested, not willingly she had to admit to herself. She wanted to know how Rori was but more importantly how he ended up down there. This was their property and while others were free to roam it, they were not free to destroy it.

None of the siblings saw the man standing in the shadows, an angry look on his face as he watched the activity around the hole. He had found it and then found Rori but had to disappear into the darkness as the father and son had approached.

Nobody saw the father and son returning and then stopping, shock on their faces as they watched the activity around the hole. The son, Leroy junior by name, had finally convinced his father that they could use that man as he described him in their activities. Leroy senior had finally nodded and turned them back towards where Rori was. They had not expected to find help there or to see Rori raised to the surface, fastened as he was to a backboard.

Ezra, the senior paramedic on duty, had simply dropped down into the hole or pit or whatever it was. There was not a lot of room for him to maneuver at the bottom but he managed as best as he could. He stared at Rori for a moment, trying to determine just what had happened and how Rori had ended up in the hole before he shrugged. Ezra worked as best as he could to fasten Rori to the backboard, a neck collar in place before he tugged at the rope for the willing and many hands above him to raise it. He reached for the extended hands that pulled him back to the surface and then was on his knees helping to assess Rori.

Bill Buckley, lead detective for the town of Elmton, watched closely as he walked towards Rori. He had not expected to be called out for this but he should have, he decided. After all, Rori's sister had been through what was termed as an adventure even though these adventures were life and death in nature. He had been through one himself as had many of his friends. Bill had prayed that no one else would have one but that didn't seem to help. He sighed. God was in control, he knew, and he also had to acknowledge that God was leading each one of them into a deeper relationship with Himself through it all.

Brit looked up as she sensed someone stopping in front of her and sighed. Of course, Bill would be here. Who else would come, right? She sighed deeper.

"We found him, Bill, down in that hole." Brit pointed at the pit. "It wasn't there last week when we were through it. So, who dug it and why?"

Bill shook his head, staring around the area. He had no idea who would have done just that. It was a remote area of the quarry and not one that many people would transverse.

"Did you see anyone at all?" Bill waited patiently for the three to study one another and then study him before they shook their heads.

"We didn't, Bill." Bevan spoke for his sisters and himself. They were that close that they could almost read one another's minds. "Why would Rori be down there?"

Bill shrugged. He had no idea why Rori was there or even how he got there. A patrol officer had passed by Rori's home at Bill's request. Rori's truck was in his driveway. That didn't explain how Rori had arrived at the quarry or was down in that pit. Bill's head raised as he sensed that they were being watched and that by more than one party. This was not how the day was to go. He was due to leave that evening for a week's holiday with his wife and two children. That leaving now seemed in doubt to some extent.

"You've given your statements?" At their collective nods, Bill turned for a moment as he heard the conversation behind him and watched as the backboard that Rori was fastened to was raised and then carried towards the parking lot. It was not an easy trail for the men to walk but they did it willingly. "Okay. I'm away next week but Jason or Lily will be in touch. Now, head off. I'm not leaving you here for now. It's a crime scene."

Brit nodded before she walked away, following the men and women surrounding Rori. This was not how her day was to have been spent. The siblings had decided that they needed a day out in nature and the quarry was a favourite spot for that. She shifted her backpack to a more comfortable position, feeling watched as she did so. And that watcher meant her harm. All Brit could do was pray for Rori and then for protection for herself and her siblings. She wanted no harm to come to them. And that was just was she was afraid would happen.

"Brit?" Becc reached for her sister's hand, needing that contact with her. "Who dug that hole?"

"I don't know, Becc, and I don't know why. Likely to try and trap some animal. Only Rori ended up in it." Brit bit at her lip. "Come on, guys. Let's head for the hospital. Just maybe we can find out how he is."

Brit shifted on her uncomfortable seat in the waiting room at the hospital Emergency Room, staring around at all the people who seemed to be sick and needed to be there. She had watched as Richard and Raleigh had arrived, Rori being Raleigh's brother. Brit sighed. Her siblings had headed off to other activities, leaving her on her own. She was on her feet, ready to walk away, stopping as she saw Raleigh in front of her.

"Brit?" Raleigh simply reached to hug the other lady. "Thank you. Bill tells me that you and your siblings found Rori."

"We did." Brit looked around, uncomfortable with the thanks. "We were just out there for a fun day."

"And that fun day changed." Richard hugged her as well before he reached for Raleigh's hand. "Here. Let's sit for a moment. Raleigh's parents are on their way but it will take them a bit to get here."

"How is Rori?" Brit was almost afraid to ask.

"He's rousing, now that they're able to hydrate him." Raleigh sighed. "I wish I know how he ended up out there. Timothy was by his house. His truck is there. That doesn't explain much."

Chapter 3

Brit moved restlessly on her seat, not even sure if she should still be there. Raleigh and Richard watched her closely before exchanging glances. Brit needed to be there, they decided, before Richard was on his feet, heading for his in-laws. Ross and Rebekah had appeared, searching for Raleigh. Richard hugged them and then sent them towards his wife, turning as he heard more footsteps and his security team appeared.

"What do we know, Richard?" Timothy spoke for the four.

"Not a lot. Rori was found in a hole in the ground. We don't know for how long he was there." Richard was worried about Rori before he saw his own brother, Riley, approaching him.

"That's not good." Silver moved past him to where Raleigh was on her feet, greeting her parents. She frowned as she saw Brit standing off to the side before she threw a look back at Richard, seeing his head give a slight shake.

"Who found him?" This from Stephen, who was monitoring the foot traffic around them.

"Brit Morrison and her siblings. I need to speak with her but right now, the focus is on Rori." Richard moved away as he saw the nurse approaching Rori's parents. His hand reached for Raleigh's as he approached her.

"This way. The physician is with Rori but asked that you come in so that he can speak with you." The nurse stopped at a room, pointing into it. She watched with compassion as the two ladies had trouble keeping their composure.

Rebekah stood for a moment at Rori's bedside before her hand was out and touching his hair, as dirty and debris-filled as it seemed. He moved restlessly, his eyelids flickering but not opening completely. Ross watched his son, leaning closer to try and understand the mutterings that came from his son. He frowned at Rebekah before he was away, looking for Bill.

"Bill?" Ross stopped in front of his son's friend. "What happened to Rori?"

Bill stared past Ross for a moment before his attention came back to him.

"We don't know, Ross. Brit and her siblings found him in that hole. We have no idea how long he was down there or why." Bill's smile was compassionate as he watched Ross struggle to compose himself. This was not what was needed, Bill knew, another child going through danger.

"I see." Ross turned to find Brit, seeing that the lady had disappeared. "Where did she go to?"

"Home, Ross." Silver, one of Richard's security team, had approached, not to listen in but to provide security for her friend's father. "We'll catch up with her."

"We will." Ross turned back to where his wife was waiting, not sure where he should be at this point.

"Ross? The physician will be around shortly. He wants to speak with all of us." Rebekah reached to hug her husband, turning them back towards Rori.

Raleigh sighed. Rori was not to have been hurt or go through anything like what she and Richard had. They had been forced to marry when Richard had been injured. Despite that, they were deeply in love. Rori had provided support for them both as had Riley but both Richard and Raleigh had prayed that her brother not be injured or in danger. God had willed otherwise, she thought. How do we find out who it is and why before he is injured any further? A thought had her turning towards the door, wondering at where Brit was. She needed to be there. Rori needed to know who had found him.

Rori's family walked away from his hospital room late that night. There had been no real answers as to how he was. The physician could not explain why he had no injuries but was not responsive. Nothing showed up in the blood panels that would explain that.

Ross was reluctant to leave, turning in the doorway to study his son. He sighed. There had to be someone out there who could explain why Rori was like he was. Bill had shrugged when he was questioned by the family. He had no answers and plainly told them that.

Early in the morning, Rori was roused by a hand shaking his shoulder. He sat up, blinking at the man standing by his bedside. He nodded and regretted it as his head began to pound. Rori took the bag of clothes that he was handed and headed for the bathroom, staggering as he did so. He sighed. He wanted to sleep but whoever it was out there? They seemed determined that he not.

Opening the door, Rori squinted around the room, feeling a hand on his arm that led him away from the hospital room and to the outside. He was shoved not too gently into a vehicle before the truck sped away from the hospital. Rori didn't realize the fear and consternation that was left in his wake.

Ross stared at the charge nurse in shock before he almost ran to Rori's room. She was correct. Rori had disappeared. Not one person had seen him leave or who had taken him away. Bill had been called in, bringing Jason, his fellow detective, with him. They had searched the hospital as well before standing in the security room and watching the video. They could see Rori being led from the room and then from the hospital. They just could not determine who had done it. That man had kept his head tucked into the hood of a jacket. And the truck had been positioned in such a way so that the license plate could not be seen.

Bill walked back towards Ross who stood outside Rori's room, a frown on his face. He had no answers as to why this had happened or who it was.

"Ross? Who did Rori anger?" Bill had to ask that question as part of the investigation.

"Rori? Anger someone? I can't see that, Bill. He works his art with the glass blowing, leaving me to look after the office work for the most part. He is very talented that way." Ross blew out a frustrated breath. "Is his artwork why he was taken?"

"We don't know that, Ross. This investigation is in the preliminary stages." Bill bowed his head to pray for his friend and his family, knowing that God was in control. "Head on home, Ross. I'll be around later today. If you think of anything at all that might help, call or text me."

Ross walked away, his steps slow and somewhat unsteady. He didn't see the police officer who walked beside him, a hand out to help him. Bill watched him before he turned away, heading for his own car and then the office. This was not how this was to go but he knew from his own experience with his wife and those of his friends who had shared adventures that this would only get worse. He headed for Brit's home, seeing it in darkness, her car parked in the driveway before he headed back to the department. He had work to do on other cases and this with Rori was just one of many.

Chapter 4

Brit lifted her head from her pillow close to the middle of the night, frowning. She was on her feet and dressed before she crept through her home, going window to window, trying to make sense of what she was hearing. She sighed. Someone was out there and she needed to call in the authorities. Only she had no proof that someone wanted into her home or to harm her.

A sound at her back door had Brit spinning and then creeping that way. She didn't make it to the mudroom before she saw dark forms running her way. Her scream split through the air in the home before a hand was clapped across her mouth and then another arm was wrapped around her abdomen, trapping her arms to her sides. She struggled to escape, not able to not matter how much her body twisted and turned. Her screams were muffled by the hand across her mouth. Brit was terrified to say the least, not knowing who had her in his grasp.

Brit was carried through the broken door and to a vehicle that sat on a street behind her home. Her abductors had no problem walking through the yards, knowing that people would be asleep and that their dark forms would not show clearly on any security system. The night was cloudy, the moon and stars only peeking out briefly before they were covered once more by the scudding dark clouds.

Shoved into a vehicle, Brit was unable to move, sandwiched as she was between the two men who joined her on the back seat. Each one grasped her wrist, preventing her from moving too far, the seatbelt preventing her from rising and trying to escape over them.

Brit's heart stuttered in her chest as she twisted to stare behind her as the vehicle sped off, screeching tires leaving dark marks on the street pavement. A man from one of the houses ran to the edge of the road to see what had happened or to try and get a glimpse of the vehicle. He just couldn't see anything but the dust that lingered in the night air. He frowned and then shrugged. Likely just some teens showing off, he decided, not knowing how wrong he was.

Her eyes closing against the tears that she refused to shed, Brit prayed as she had never prayed before. God, where are You? Please? Let me go free and go home. She still struggled to escape but to no avail. A blindfold suddenly dropped over her vision and caused her to scream once more, fear sending chills through her.

"Be quiet!" The harsh voice from the man to her right sounded in the silence that followed her scream. "Be quiet or you'll pay for your screams!"

Brit sank back against the seat, not willing to be hurt any more than she had been. She could feel the pain from the tight grip on her wrists, knowing that she would have bruises there once she was released.

The four men shared a glance before the driver increased his speed, not seeing the patrol vehicle that passed him and then spun to follow, the lights and sirens activated as the officer sped after then.

"We need to shake him." The front passenger twisted to watch behind them. "Slow down and try one of our usual tricks."

The driver nodded, slowing the vehicle and then pulling off to the side of the road. The four men watched as the officer didn't walk towards them right away.

"What's he waiting for?" The rear passenger on Brit's left questioned the actions of the man.

"Likely running the plates." The driver suddenly reversed, sending his car into the patrol vehicle and sending that vehicle down an embankment before he accelerated away from the scene. He had no care or concern that he had hurt a law enforcement officer. The man beside Brit clapped a hand across her mouth as she screamed once more.

"Shut up!" His coarse voice grated against her senses and she grew silent, not willing to draw his ire against her any more than she had.

Spinning his wheel, the driver headed across town and then into the industrial park that lined the edge of the city limits. He pulled up to a well-kept building, waiting for the large door to roll up before he pulled into the garage area of the building. He turned the car off before he was out of the vehicle and heading rapidly for the office area.

Brit waited, fear uppermost in her mind. She had no idea who these men were or what they wanted. Fear kept her motionless, even when the men slid from the seat beside her. She was too afraid to reach for the blindfold or to even try to escape.

The three men paced, waiting for the driver to return. They had no idea why they had been sent to bring Brit to their employer. They knew that he already had a man in custody. That man was not awakening as he should and that was angering their boss.

The driver returned, simply pointing at the vehicle. Two of the men reached inside and dragged a protesting Brit from the car, walking her rapidly towards a door across the garage from where the truck sat. One of them punched in a code and watched as the door slowly opened. Brit was manhandled inside even as she was struggling to escape and protesting at the rough treatment.

Shoved down a flight of stairs, Brit lost her balance and fell, landing heavily on the concrete floor. She whimpered slightly from the pain and scrapes that she knew that she would have on her knees and hands before she was hauled to her feet and shoved forward, a hand on her upper arm keeping her to her feet.

Brit could hear the mutters of the men with her but couldn't understand their words. She felt them pause for a moment and heard the sound of a lock turning and the squeak of an opening door. Shoved violently forward, Brit once more landed on her hands and knees, a soft cry of pain drawn from her even as the door slammed behind her and the lock sounded loudly as it was turned, sealing her into the room.

Shifting to a sitting position, Brit waited for what seemed an eternity before she finally reached to pull the blindfold from her face. She blinked in the light, her eyes narrowing as they adjusted to the light. Brit stared around the stark room, seeing two bunks, a table and chairs, and catching sight of a washroom through an open doorway.

On her feet, Brit searched for a way out, stopping in shock as she approached the bunks. On her knees, she reached for the body lying on one, turning the man to his back. Sitting back in shock, Brit stared at Rori, seeing the marks of abuse on him.

"Rori?" Brit touched his face lightly before she was on her feet, running for the washroom and to find a cloth or towel or something that she could dunk into warm water and wring out. Back beside him, Brit carefully touched his face, washing away what she could of the dirt and blood that covered his face. "Rori? What did they do to you?"

Rori roused slightly, feeling the softness of Brit's hands as she touched his face before he sank back into the blackness that seemed to be his only world at the moment. He couldn't rouse enough to determine who was with him nor could he rouse enough to pray. His only thought was that God had freed him somehow. He didn't want a lady with him, not to face the brutality of his captors.

Brit sank to a sitting position beside the bunk, a hand on Rori's arm. She prayed for release but more so, she prayed for Rori to awaken and tell her that they were okay and that he knew how to get away. She just didn't think that would happen.

Chapter 5

Raleigh paused as she approached Richard, ducking under the arm that he held out and then wrapped around her. She was so afraid for Rori. They had been searching for him, just not finding him. Richard had driven them by Brit's house, stopping as he saw the police vehicles surrounding it.

"Brit?" Raleigh didn't ask more. She didn't have to.

"Brit. We have no idea what's going on." Richard was away from Raleigh, walking towards the police line, waiting for someone he knew to look around.

Bill turned as he heard a new vehicle stopping and acknowledged Richard with a slight lifting of his hand. He turned back to Jason, both of them heading into the house. He had been called in by the patrol officer who had walked around Brit's home and found the broken-in door. The officer had walked through the house, not finding Brit, concerned as she had been threatened that day. Word had reached the officers on the street that Brit was to disappear and not be seen again.

"Thomas? What do you have?" Bill's head was turning as he studied the damage to the door and watched the crime scene techs working away to find what evidence that they could.

"Not a lot. Brit's not here, Bill. I would say that she disappeared really early." Thomas was frustrated.

He was a friend of Bevan's and knew how worried Bevan would be to know that Brit had disappeared.

"Early?" Bill shook his head. That figures, he decided. Take her before anyone could see anything and disappear with her. "You're talking with the neighbours?"

"We have been. No one heard anything at all, not that they will admit to at any rate."

Bill frowned at how Thomas had worded his response.

"That's an interesting way to describe that, Thomas. Any reason or just a hunch?"

"Just a hunch, Bill. Breaking in the door would have sounded loud at night. Her neighbour to the left is close. Their bedroom is on this side of the house. And they were home." Thomas frowned as he thought through what the man had said. "Somehow, I think he knows something and is just not wanting to get involved."

"That's highly possible." Bill walked away, searching through the house. He sighed. This is not how the day was to be, he decided. He now had to reach out to Brit's family and he also knew that Raleigh and Richard would want answers, answers that he just didn't have.

Raleigh watched Bill as he headed for his vehicle and then just drove away. Richard wrapped an arm tighter around her, knowing how distressed she was. He didn't want that for her but there didn't seem to be any other option.

"What did he find, Richard?" Raleigh rubbed at her abdomen, their unborn child active at the moment.

"I don't know, sweetheart. I really don't know. He'll talk to her siblings and then they'll reach out to us. Rori and Brit are connected somehow. I just don't know how." He sighed. "I reached out to Abe and Emma to see what they could do." Abe ran a security team as well and his wife, Emma, had a business that tracked and found people and places. Emma just couldn't explain how she did that, only stating that God led her.

"Thanks. Let's head for home. We're not finding anything here." Raleigh bit at her lip. "Is there anything at Rori's?"

"We'll head there before going home. The team is training but Stephen has been in touch. They're working it as they can." Richard shut the truck door after Raleigh before he stood and stared around. He nodded at Jason who was still on site before he walked slowly around and climbed behind the wheel. All he could do at present was pray for his brother-in-law and the lady who seemed to have become part of it all.

Bevan stared at Bill as he stood in his kitchen, an arm around Becc. The siblings were horrified to hear that Brit had disappeared from her home without much evidence as to who.

"It was early?" Becc could barely get out the words.

"It seems to be, Becc. When did you two last speak with her?" Bill's notebook was out as he made his notes.

"Last night, around nine, I think." Becc rubbed at her face. "We had plans to have lunch today." She looked up at Bevan, seeing the distress and worry that he was trying hard to hide and not succeeding very well. "Bevan?"

"I spoke with her around 10. She was heading for bed, she said. I was supposed to be out of town today but the trip was called off early this morning." Bevan paled as he reached for his phone. "I don't know who this was that arranged it but my employer asked me to go. Here's the contact information." He sent it to Bill's phone. "Do you think this was a plant or a way to get me out of town while they kidnapped her?"

Bill stared at his phone, recognizing the name. He nodded before he looked up, a shuttered look on his face.

"I would say that it was. I recognize the name. He's been under investigation for years but we could never prove anything." All the investigators over the years had been frustrated at that.

"And it falls to Brit to do that." Bevan walked away, angry that his sister had become involved in something like this.

Becc watched her brother before she spoke. Bill could hear the real fear in her voice.

"How do we find them, Bill?"

"That's a good question, Becc. I don't have an answer for you. We continue to investigate and run down the leads that come in. We go to the street and talk to our contacts there. We'll find them."

"But will they be dead or alive when you do so?" Becc walked away as well, tears flowing down her face, to find Bevan waiting to simply hug his sister.

Bill stood for a moment, his eyes on the siblings before he walked away, frustrated that Brit had disappeared and that they had no immediate answer as to why or even where they were.

Chapter 6

Richard paced his home office, his eyes on Raleigh as she slumped on the couch there, sound asleep. She had not been sleeping well lately, and he didn't want to awaken her if he could help him. He could see the signs of stress on her face and in how she was sitting. They had been through enough, Richard thought, with what his team had faced and then themselves.

"Raleigh?" Richard simply sat beside her and swept her into his arms. "What are your thoughts?"

"My thoughts? They are so muddled at the moment that they are not making sense. I don't understand why Rori. What did he do to anyone? He's an artist, a glassblower. It's a highly skilled art that he's been working on since he was a child. Dad let him. There should be nothing there other than perhaps jealousy by someone else that would warrant him being taken." Raleigh snuggled closer to Richard, feeling his love and caring for her in how he was holding her. "What do you think?"

Richard paused before he spoke, praying for his beloved bride and her brother and their family. The family didn't need this, not at all. Nor did Brit's siblings.

"I can see that easily, love, but who would it be? That group is a small group here in the area." Richard rubbed at his cheek, not sure what to say or how to continue.

"It is. It could be someone from outside of the area. Dad and Rori's work is well known. They ship all over the country and even outside of it." Raleigh sighed. "We're no further ahead in figuring this out, are we?"

"No, we're not. We're all working on it as are Emma and Abe. Don and his team are weighing in as well." Richard named friends who had security teams as well. Emma also had a business where she found people and information that no one else could.

"That's good. I just want Rori home and safe. Somehow, I don't know if that will happen very quickly." Raleigh slept, her emotions getting the better of her.

Richard watched as she slept, raising his head as he heard a tap at the door and then his brother, Riley, appeared, simply sitting in companionship with the couple. Richard nodded at his brother, accepting the fact that he was there and not where he should be. He had been there when Richard and Raleigh faced their adventure just as Richard had been there when Riley and Rayleen had faced theirs.

Bill turned as he heard his name called. A colleague, Lily Gordon, was running towards him.

"Bill? Can we talk?" Lily slid to a halt before she hugged Bill and then pointed towards a diner nearby.

"We can. I'm not sure that I understand why you're here and not at work." Bill slid into the booth across from Lily, waiting for her to speak.

"I have word, Bill. Someone approached me and told me where they are. I'm not sure if they'll still be there by the time you get your warrants and search the building." Lily slid a slip of paper across the table to him. "I won't tell you who."

Bill nodded, knowing Lily from working as an officer and fellow detective for years. She was not transitioning to working as the director of the woman's shelter and was highly protective of those ladies even as she continued as a detective at the present time.

"I understand." He slipped the paper into his shirt pocket. "What do you know, Lily?"

Lily shrugged. She knew little, she had to admit, other than that the couple were still in town. She had suspicions as to who was behind it but without any solid proof, she would not say. That proof was what she was searching for and finding it difficult to obtain.

"I don't know much other than that, Bill. I have suspicions but nothing that I can say at the moment." Lily was on her feet and walking rapidly away, leaving Bill to stare at her untouched cup of coffee. He looked up as he sensed someone sitting across from him. Stephen, from Richard's team, sat there. "Stephen?"

"Bill? Do you know where they are? We want to relieve Raleigh's worry if we can."

"I know that you do. And no, we don't know where they are. That's frustrating for us all."

"It is. All we can do is pray for them. And pray for those who hold them." Stephen nodded at the look that Bill shot him. "We have to, Bill. We are told to pray for our enemies."

Bill sighed. Stephen was just so right, he thought. Enemies were to be prayed for.

Walking back towards the department, Bill was lost in thought, not seeing the shadow that he had picked up. The two men shared a look before they ran towards Bill. Hearing running footsteps, Bill turned but was not quick enough to avoid the bat that was swung at him. An arm came up to partially block the strike but he was not successfully in that. He slumped to the ground, consciousness fading even as the two men ran from the scene. Bill didn't hear the shouts of alarm or feel the hands of fellow officers as they reached to assist him.

Andrew McBeth, the police chief, stood from his desk as Jason appeared in his doorway, shocked to hear that Bill had been assaulted and was unconscious.

"Where is he?" Andrew was moving from his office, the door shut and locked behind him.

"On his way to the hospital. I reached out to Phoebe and she's on her way to look after his kids. An officer is heading for Cora."

Andrew paced the hallway outside of the cubicle where Bill was laying. He had had no word yet on the extent of Bill's injuries. He worried about his friend and fellow officer. They had been through a lot over the years together. This was not what they needed.

Jason approached Andrew, his eyes shifting between his chief and the cubicle curtain.

"How is he?" His voice was kept low.

"I'm still waiting to hear." Andrew shot a look towards the doors to the waiting room. "Cora's out there?"

"She is. Raleigh and Rayleen are with her." Jason walked away, his shoulders slumping. The weight of the investigation into Brit and Rori's disappearance would now rest on him. He turned as he felt an hand stop him. Sam, a newly-promoted detective and good friend, stood there.

"Jason? I'm to work with you on this. What can you tell me?"

Jason shrugged, his eyes on his friend. Just like Jason, Sam had grown up in Elmton.

"We need to discuss this, Sam. Let's head back to the office. Andrew will call with word." Jason's heart was sore for his friends. All he could do was pray for them.

Chapter 7

After days of being unconscious or not conscious enough to be aware of where he was or what had happened to him, Rori roused slowly. He sat up, his feet on the dirty, garbage-strewn floor without knowing how dirty the room was. He was on his feet, heading for a door and finding it locked. Rori frowned at that before he felt along the wall, his hand on that wall the only thing keeping him on his feet. Opening another door, he stared at the rudimentary bathroom before he had the water turned on to reach as hot as he could stand it. Water splashed on his face, not really helping to wake him up. Rori turned at last, heading back into the room, his eyes squinting as he tried to focus.

His legs hit a bed and he swayed as he came to a sudden stop, barely standing. He sat before he was laying down, pulling a dirty and torn blanket over himself. Rori froze as he felt something beside him. Reaching out a shaking and tentative hand, he frowned. There was someone lying there. He raised up enough to realize that it was a lady whom he knew. Why was Brit there? And just where was there? He simply reached to wrap her into his arms, seeking solace from her presence and desperate to know why they were there. Even when he whispered her name, there was no response from her. Rori's eyes closed as he slept, not hearing the door unlock and open.

The man who had taken the couple captive stood in the doorway, an evil sneer on his face. He frowned at the dimness of the room, not sure where the couple were but knowing that they had not escaped. They would not. He had a plan to use them for vengeance and not one person would stand in his way. He locked the door behind him once more, not seeing Brit's head raise for a moment before it dropped back down.

Brit was on her feet the next morning or what she assumed to be morning, seeking a way out. Something was driving her to this. She paused at the window, looking out as best that she could through the dirty panes. They were on the first floor, with not that great of a drop to the ground. Brit jumped and stifled a scream as she felt an arm around her. Turning, she stared at Rori as he stood there, swaying back and forth, the only thing seeming to hold him upright his arm around her.

"Rori? Should you be on your feet?" Brit kept her voice low, not sure if there were microphones or whatever in the room.

"I have to be." Rori squinted at the lady beside him. "Brit? Where are we?"

"Not where we want to be." Brit's words were bit out, anger and fear driving that. "We're being held captive by someone. And you have not been awake that much." She looked behind her at the locked door. "We need to leave."

"We do." Rori stiffened his knees to try and keep his balance. "We can get out of this window?"

"I think so. It's not that far to the ground." Brit frowned as she saw a figure appear and then gave a grim smile. "We have help, Rori. Someone has found us." She worked at the window, not letting Rori help. She frowned at him, knowing that he was barely staying on his feet.

The window finally raised and Brit slipped through it, hands reaching to help her before they reached to help Rori.

"This way, you two." The undercover officer and the man from the streets quickly moved the couple away from the house. The window had been lowered once more. "We were ready to move into the house."

"He's not there?" Brit was surprised but worried about her friend. Rori just didn't seem to be able to move as well as he should. "What did they do to Rori?"

"I'm not sure." The undercover officer, Brent by name, knew full well what had happened to Rori. He needed to reach out to Bill or one of the detectives and quickly. He was afraid that Rori would disappear once more. And this time? He would not be coming back to his family.

"I know you know." Brit's words were spit out at Brent, causing him to smile briefly. "We need to get him to help. Only who do we turn to?"

"I have someone, Brit. We'll get you both there. We need you to be examined as well." Brent rushed them to a dilapidated looking vehicle.

Brit dug in her heels. There was no way that vehicle could even move.

"In, Brit." Brent almost shoved her inside to land on the back seat beside Rori. He took off as soon as he was behind the wheel, not even worrying about his seatbelt.

Brit's mouth opened and then closed. He must know what he's doing, she decided. Her eyes were on Rori, seeing the stress and illness that coloured it. Rori was not doing well and she had no idea why. Her thoughts then turned to her brother and sister, praying that they were safe. She opened her mouth to ask and then snapped it closed. She would find out at some point, she knew. Right now? Getting them both to safety was what was needed the most.

Watching carefully as he sped away from the building, Brent knew that it was only a matter of time until it was discovered that Rori and Brit had escaped. They would be searched for. No one knew why they had been taken or what the plans were but Brent doubted that it was for their health.

Brent headed for his own home, that sat next to Rori's home. Rori and he were friends and classmates. It had disturbed him to no end when Rori had disappeared, not once but twice. He had been out there searching along with the others, keeping to the shadows as much as he could. No one had been successful in finding him the first time until Brit and her siblings had stumbled upon him. No one could explain why he was in that pit.

Brit kept a watch on Brent, recognizing him as well. She frowned. He was a police officer, she knew. Just how had he stumbled upon them? Or had God led that way? Brit breathed out a soft prayer of praise and then for help. Her arm was tight around Rori, knowing that he was just not himself and almost unconscious again. She needed him to be alert and to tell her what was going on. Brit had no clue.

"Brent? Where are we heading?" Brit finally asked the question that had been burning at the tip of her tongue.

"My place. I'll hide you there for now and get word to Bill." Brent pulled into his garage, the door closing swiftly behind him. He shifted to stare at the couple. "He's not doing good, is he?"

"No, he's not. I couldn't get him to wake up until just before we climbed out of that window." Brit frowned. "Although when I woke up, he was holding me. He had to have been on his feet at some point."

Brent shot her a quick glance before studying his friend. He nodded. Rori had claimed Brit for his own. He searched his memory, nodding as he remembered the looks and the way that Rori had studied Brit when they were in school. Interest had been there but Rori had not acted on it.

Chapter 8

His arm around Brent's shoulder, Rori shuffled into the house, his feet raising slowly and unsteadily as he climbed the few steps up to the main portion of the house. He paused, his breath difficult to gather before he nodded. Brent simply walked him to the living room and gently shoved him to the couch.

Brit was beside him, an arm around him as she tried to assess him, knowing that was not what she could do. She was worried about her friend and could only pray for him.

"Brent? We need a doctor for him. Who can we call?" Brit chewed at her lip, trying to come up with a name.

Brent was nodding. He had already reached out to a trusted friend, one who had helped Brent in the past.

"Josh will be here shortly. He'll assess both of you for Bill. We need that. Then, we'll make a decision of what to do for Rori." Brent sighed. That was the rub, he decided. What do they do for them?

"Josh? Of course. He'll do that." Brit was on her feet, heading for the kitchen. "Brent? We need to get fluid in to him. What do you have?"

"I have some broth in the freezer." Brent reached for it, setting it into the microwave to thaw and heat. "And there's water and also juice." Brent's hand reached for her. "What can I do for you, Brit?"

Brit stared at him before she shrugged. She had no idea what he could do. She blinked back tears, her stress level higher than it had ever been.

"I need to let Bevan and Becc know that I am okay. We need to reach out to Raleigh, too." She sighed. "And we need to talk to Bill or one of them."

"We will. Bill knows that I have you two safe." Brent grinned at her. "For now? Bailey left some clothes here the last time she stayed. You're about the same size as her. Second door on the right, Brit. Go and have a shower and get into clean clothes. It will help to some extent to make you feel more you."

Brit nodded. She was still highly puzzled by what had happened. It made no sense that Rori would have disappeared. As a glass blower artist, his work could not be used for anything illegal, she didn't think. She paled enough and swayed, causing Brent to reach for her arm.

"Brit?" Brent waited patiently for her to speak.

"It's not about Rori, is it? It's about me. We were friends in high school and have continued that to some extent. It's me. I'm a gemologist. That's what they're after, and they're using Rori to get to me." Brit ran from the kitchen, heading for the room that she had been directed to, barely able to see for the tears flowing down her face and clouding her vision.

Brent stared after her for a moment before he headed for the door. Opening it, he found both Bill and Josh standing there and staring at him.

"Guys? Come on in." Brent stepped outside for a moment, seeing nothing that alarmed him as of yet. That could change in a moment, he well knew.

"Where are they?" Bill just asked his question, knowing that Brent would respond as he could. "You said they were safe?"

"They are." Brent pointed towards the living room, watching as Josh had already disappeared that way. "Rori's in the living room. Brit is in one of the bedrooms, getting cleaned up. I found them escaping from a building earlier and brought them here. Rori is not really aware of what is going on. Brit is angry and also confused and terrified. She thinks it's been her all along and that whoever it was? They were using Rori to get to her."

Bill nodded. That had been something that the detectives had been tossing back and forth over the last day or so. As a gemologist, Brit would be the natural one to take and try and force into criminal activities.

"I see. You know, with Rori's work, they could put small gems into it and they would not really be noticed." Bill looked past Brent at Brit, seeing her nod of understanding. "Brit? We need to talk."

"We do." She disappeared towards the kitchen, leaving the two men staring after her until Brent turned at a call from Josh.

Bill followed Brit, praying for the young woman who now seemed to be having an adventure with a friend of his, an adventure that none of them wanted this couple to embark on. They knew that God was walking with that couple but it still stung that another friend was going through this.

"Brit?" Bill took the mug of coffee offered him and then pointed to the table. "Sit, please. We need to talk. But first, let me pray with you."

When Brit lifted her head at last, her eyes were on the doorway to the hall. She could hear quiet conversation coming from that way, a tone of concern and worry underlying the words.

"What do you need to know, Bill?"

"Tell me what happened to you." Bill's pen was posed over his notepad as he watched Brit closely.

Brit shrugged, not sure exactly what to say. She simply stated what had happened.

"I don't know the men, Bill. And I can't describe them. Ask me to describe a gem that I caught a glimpse of and I can. These men? I can't do that. I'm sorry." Brit was on her feet, almost running towards where Rori was.

Josh looked around, assessing Brit as he did so.

"Brit? Where you hurt in any way?" Josh waited patiently for her to speak.

Brit shook her head.

"Physically? No. But in any other way? I am. I feel like a shattered jewel, do you know that? And you can't put a shattered jewel back together the way it was." Brit shook in fear for a moment, finding Brent's arm around her and directing her to a seat in a chair near Rori. "How's Rori?"

"I don't know for sure, Brit. It is concerning that he is not awakening as he should. Was he able to say anything?" Josh looked up at Bill, who stood nearby, a shuttered look on his face as he studied Rori.

"No, he didn't. I don't understand. I know that he was up at some point. I woke up earlier wrapped in his arms. He doesn't do that to the ladies. So why me?" Brit was genuinely puzzled but in the deep recesses of her heart, the teenager that she had had a crush on had just awakened the desire for a relationship with the man whom he had become.

"To protect you, more than likely, Brit. Even if he was not aware of where he was or what had happened, it is ingrained in us guys to protect the ladies." Bill gave a brief and grim smile before he walked away.

Chapter 9

Richard stood on his front porch that afternoon, watching as Bill trudged towards him. That was the only word that Richard could think of to describe how Bill was moving. He grew more worried about Rori and yes, Brit, as Bill walked towards him. He didn't think that there would be good news at all.

"Bill?" Richard's voice brought Bill's head up and he gave a smile.

"Richard? I'm sorry. I'm here at your mealtime." Bill walked up the steps, fatigue evident in every step.

"That's never a problem. Come and share with us." Richard walked back into the house, finding Raleigh waiting for him as well as the rest of their families. "We'll share a meal and then pray. I sense that you have news."

"I do." Bill hesitated for a moment, searching all the faces turned to him, seeing the hope and yet fear on them all. "Rori is safe."

Raleigh stared at Bill even as she felt Richard's arms around her.

"I'm sorry, Bill. What did you say?" Her voice was barely audible even as hope sprung in her heart and the hearts of the rest of the families.

"Rori is safe. I have seen him but not spoken with him." Bill nodded at them all. "First, may we eat and then spend time in prayer? He and Brit will need that and need that very much."

At last, heads were raised as they all turned to Bill.

"What can you tell us, Bill?" Ross Reade spoke for the group. "Only what you can, though."

"I can't tell you a lot. Sometime this morning, Rori was aware enough that he and Brit were able to escape. Someone found them and got them to safety. Right now, they are with Brent and will stay there for the next day or so. I won't let you go to them. Not until I've had a chance to speak with Rori. That hasn't been possible yet." Bill gave what details he could before he walked away, heading for his own home and Cora and their two children.

The families stared at one another before they all began to speak. Ross' hand went up to silence the group.

"We don't know what happened or why." Ross looked around at Riley who had made a sound. "Riley? Your thoughts?"

"Brit would have been taken to use for her knowledge of gems. Rori? He could have been taken to get to her. She is known not to refuse to help anyone. It doesn't explain where he was though and how he ended up in that pit." They were still all puzzled by that fact.

"It doesn't make a lot of sense." Raleigh looked around as Riley made a sound. "Riley?"

"Brit and her siblings are known to walk that path a lot, at least once a week. If someone wanted to get to Brit, they would use that fact. They would have time to dig a hole, bringing in equipment to do so and hiding the evidence. They drop Rori down there when he's not awake and wait." Riley was sure of his facts. He just couldn't prove them.

Ross was nodding. Riley was correct, he decided.

"I think you're on to something, Riley. So, how do we prove that and then determine who is behind this? From what little Bill has been able to say, they don't have a lot of evidence."

"No, they don't." Richard was frustrated at that, knowing the evidence would have been hidden by the weather before Rori disappeared. "Do we know when Rori disappeared?" His arm was tight around Raleigh.

"We don't know for sure, Richard." Reynold Ransome spoke up. "I know that you are trying to determine that as is your team and also your friends. There just isn't enough information there to determine that."

"No, there isn't, Dad, and there should be. We've gone through his home and his work building with Ross. I don't know that he was taken from either place. His truck is at his home but that doesn't mean that's where he was." Richard rubbed at his cheek, frowning at the table as he did so. They were missing that one crucial piece of information that would solve this. And he didn't know if Rori would remember at all or remember in time to help them.

"I spoke with Rori about four days before he disappeared." Riley spoke up. "We were to meet for lunch the next day but he called to cancel. He had something come up, he said, and had to be out of town. Does anyone know why?" He looked around at the families gathered in the room, shock on most of their faces.

"He disappeared that night then or the next day." Richard's eyes slid closed. "As we didn't know that. Ross? Did he come in to work or call in?"

Ross was shaking his head.

"He had taken a week's vacation and was planning on doing some day trips in the area. He was known for that, not leaving home overnight if he could help it." Ross' head dropped for a moment as he prayed for his son. "Now, how do we determine when and how?"

Bill had walked back into the room, having had to leave to take a call. He sighed. This was what they had needed but had not had. He couldn't blame the families. It was what it was. It wasn't the first time that information that was crucial to an investigation had not been forthcoming.

"Riley? Did he say where he was heading?" Bill just had to ask, even though he had decided that Riley not likely knew.

"No, he didn't. He usually doesn't if he really isn't sure what he wants to do." Raleigh spoke up, her eyes locked on Riley's, who was nodding. "He likes to do day trips to pioneer villages and museums. He gets a lot of his ideas for his glass work there. He takes after Dad that way."

Her father was nodding. That was what they both did, he knew, but it didn't explain why Rori had disappeared as he had. That was something they were all working on.

Bill left soon afterwards, needing to be in the office for some interviews. He just didn't want to do that. He stood for a moment, his head tilted to the sky as he sought answers from God. All Bill could do at present was to pray for his friends. And that was something that was hard to do at the time."

Chapter 10

Rori rose at last from where he had been sleeping, rubbing at his eyes and then his face. He stared around the room, not recognizing it at all. He had no idea where he was or even what day it was for that matter. His head was somewhat clearer, Rori decided, before he reached for the clothes that were waiting for him and heading to get cleaned up. He stood at last, his hand on the door handle, before his head dropped and he began to pray. Rori had no idea what or who was on the other side of the door and that frightened him. Not much did that, he decided, before his hand pressed down on the door and he walked out of the room and into the living area of the house.

A sound from beside him had Rori spinning, fear momentarily showing on his face. He frowned at the lady who stood there, before he just reached to hug Brit. Why he did that, he had no idea but he felt drawn to her.

"Rori? Should you be up?" Brit hugged Rori before she stepped back to look up at him, wondering at his height.

"I have to, Brit. I have to. Do you know what happened to me? I can't remember and I need to." There was the sound of a lost and confused little boy in his voice.

"I don't know when you disappeared but Bevan, Becc, and I found you in a pit out in the woods. You were safe but then disappeared again. This time? I had to disappear as well. I don't know who was holding you or why." Brit frowned at the look on Rori's face and in his eyes. That look said that she was special to him.

"I was? That's strange." His arm around her, Rori turned to where he saw Brent. "Brent?"

"You're safe for now, Rori. And no, I don't know who or why either. Bill was around last night but you weren't able to speak with him. He'll be back around today at some point." Brent's hand went up. "Don't say anything, Rori, until you speak with him. I can tell you that I found you two running away from your captors." Brent turned and walked away, leaving Rori to stare after him before Brit's arm around him moved him towards the kitchen.

"You need to eat, Rori. I couldn't get any food down you when we were captive." Brit was still puzzled at how he had been holding her the day before. She knew that it was not him to do so. She stared at her hand and the ring that was there and then at Rori's hand. She remembered the ceremony, as brief as it was, and wondered if Rori would remember.

"We need to talk, Brit. Can you explain this?" Rori held up his hand. "We weren't dating. In fact, we barely spoke to one another."

Brit drew in a shaky breath. He had gone to the heart of the problem and concern.

"We were forced to marry, Rori, just like your sister and Richard. And no, I don't know why." Brit moved abruptly away from him, her phone out as a text message tone sounded. She stared down at the text before she responded to her brother that she was fine and that they would talk. She would find Bevan and Becc that afternoon. No one would stop her from finding her siblings. She needed to do that.

Brent studied the couple as they ate, a frown flickering across his face. He had no idea that they had been forced to marry. That concerned him as it made it a lot more dangerous for the couple. He knew the history of Richard and Raleigh and what had happened to them. He just didn't think that Rori and Brit would have faced the same. It was just too bizarre. A thought crossed his mind that just maybe this was all related to that but he shook his head. There was no way that it was.

Bill paused at the front door. He had returned, hopefully that he could speak with either Brit or Rori, but not sure that he could. His head dropped as he petitioned God for their safety and they would not be harmed any worse than they had been. Bill had noticed the rings the night before and had been puzzled and then greatly worried about the couple.

Brent stepped outside, his eyes on the woods around his home. He could hear the sounds of nature around his home and then turned to Bill. He simply shook his head. Brent had no answers for what they were going through, even though he knew that Bill would ask.

"Bill? Any word on what happened?" Brent kept his voice low, knowing that Rori and Brit stood just inside the door, watching the two men.

Bill shook his head. He had no answers and no one else did. He had gone to his sources on the street without any answers there.

"No one is talking, Brent. And that is unusual." Bill was puzzled at that.

"It is. Someone should be saying something at some point. Either they don't know or they are protecting someone."

"I would say that they are protecting Brit and Rori. Someone will reach out to us. And I suspect that it will go to Ev at her diner and then to us." Bill walked towards Rori, finding Rori stepping backwards, fear briefly showing on his face.

"Bill? Do you know what happened to me?" Rori had to ask.

Bill shook his head. He had no idea what was happening other than a friend was in danger.

"No, I don't, Rori. I was praying and hoping that you could tell me." Bill pointed towards the kitchen. "In there. We need to talk. You need to tell me what has happened. And yes, you do need to explain the rings."

Brit drew in a deep breath. She would have to be the one doing that, she knew. Rori had not really been aware enough of what was happening and that frustrated her. This is not how it should have been. Rori should have been able to make his own decision as to who he dated and married and that decision had been taken from the both of them.

Bill tidied away his paperwork at last, tucking the statements into a folder before locking his briefcase. He paused for a moment, his head down as he studied the dark oak table that they were sitting at. Bill looked up at last, his eyes on first Rori and then Brit. They would be going back to their lives but those very lives were now entwined in a way that no one would expect. He had no idea what God's plan or purpose was but he trusted God enough to know that He was in control of what was happening.

Rori reached for Brit's hand, finding hers grasping his tight. He shared a look with Bill and then Brent. It was up to him to protect his lady as she now was, at least for the moment. He just didn't know how he would do just that.

Chapter 11

Reaching for the door knob as the doorbell rang, Richard hesitated. He just knew that when he opened the beautiful steel door with the etched glass window, life would change for them all. He just didn't know in what way. He prayed for the families, ending his prayer in the usual "I love You".

Staring at the couple standing in front of him, Richard simply reached after a pause to hug Rori and then Brit. He didn't know what they had been through, but he could tell that it had been rough for him. He studied Rori, seeing the distress and fear that he was trying hard to hide.

"Rori? Are you okay?" Richard watched his brother-in-law as Rori hesitated and then shook his head. His eyes turned to Brit, finding that she had emotions under too tight a control. She was brittle, he decided. "Brit?"

"We'll talk, Richard. We need Brit's siblings to hear what we have to say." Rori frowned as Richard's gaze went past him and then he heard the sounds of footsteps, causing him to jump in fear.

Brit turned as she felt a hand on her back, reaching for Bevan and Becc, hugging them tightly without letting them go. Her tears began to fall as she felt Becc's sobs. They clung to one another, the younger two knowing somehow that life had changed for them and not in a good way.

"Come on in when you can." Richard turned, walking away to find Raleigh staring at him before she was through the door and hugging her brother. She knew something drastic had happened, just not what. All she could do was murmur a prayer for her brother, begging God to protect him and solve whatever it was that he was going through. And that could take time, she was well aware. It had taken time to sort out and solve what she and Richard had faced. She looked past the four standing with her to find Richard's security team and their spouses walking up the steps.

Richard looked around at all the people in his home and sighed. This was getting very old, he decided, having someone close to him in danger of dying. That was what he always feared for his friends and family. That had always been a huge concern when his team had gone out to protect others.

"Dad? Can we pray? We need that." Richard's head bowed as did everyone else's as the group simply prayed for the couple, asking for protection and peace in whatever it was they were facing. And not one person could explain what had happened, why or who was responsible.

Rori sat for a moment, Brit's hand tight in his. He could hear the murmurs from around them but his concentration was solely on Brit. She was his bride, not matter how it happened, and he would never walk away from her. Never was a long time, he was well aware, but Brit was his for life. He could feel the cracks starting in the deep control that he had on his heart. Brit was walking into his heart and life and he would not walk away from her.

Brit studied Rori, her hand tight in his, before she sighed. He would want to protect her, she knew. She had been doing that all of her life, protecting herself and then Bevan and Becc as they grew up. She didn't need someone to take over that and resented the fact that she now had that.

"Brit?" Bevan sat at his sister's feet, a hand on her arm. "Talk to us. Tell us what happened to you two."

Rori shared a look with Brit. They both knew that they had to confess to their marriage. Richard and Raleigh would understand, but would anyone else?

"This is hard, you know." Rori turned to the group. "Richard, you and Raleigh will understand best. We were forced to marry the other day. I don't remember it at all but Brit said we were given no option and no explanation. We need to find out why. I don't know where I was at first and I don't remember disappearing and from where or who had been the ones to do that. I don't really remember much else." Rori sighed once more. "We need to investigate, but I'm not sure how we can."

Shock at Rori's words showed on all the faces except for Richard and Raleigh. They would talk with the couple but later when they could be on their own. Richard reached for a pad of paper and pen, being to note what was being said. He too sighed. This would not be easy to investigate. The vibrating of his phone caught his attention and he smiled. Emma Finlay had been in touch. She had a business where she found information that no one else could. She and her husband, Abe, were good friends, Abe having a security team as well. Richard also knew that his lifelong friend, Don, would be around, his security team already reaching out to offer their help. Riley's wife's cousin, Peter, had reached out as well. He too had a security team that had helped with Riley and Rayleen's adventure near the end of it, Rayleen having been kept from her family for most of her life.

"I don't understand, Brit." Becc crowded her sister over on the couch, not caring that Brit was crammed tight to Rori. "Why would they do that?"

"We don't know, Brit. And I can't really describe the men. They took care to hide their faces as much as they could. And the minister? I somehow think that he's done this before. He wasn't surprised or scared. That much was obvious." Brit drew in a deep, shuddering breath, not sure how to explain what emotions that she was feeling. They ran too deep for her to ignore them. She studied first Becc and then Bevan, knowing that their lives had changed and not necessarily for the better. Her siblings has been threatened. That was not something that she could take lightly, not at all.

Rori's arms tightened around her as he too sought to understand what had been demanded of them. Brit had not been able to say much, not understanding much herself. His chin rested on her head, his eyes watching and studying those in the room with him. They had all been threatened, Brit had been quick to inform him. How did they then keep all of them safe? That was a question neither one of them could answer. His eyes finally locked with Richard's, who simply nodded. He knew that Richard and

Raleigh would wait to speak with them in private. Rori just didn't know how much that conversation would help.

Chapter 12

That evening, Richard paced his home, his thoughts mixed and also troubled. They had not expected to have Rori and Brit face what they were facing and what Richard and Raleigh had faced. God was in control, he had to acknowledge. It just was that it seemed too much for all of them to handle at the home.

Raleigh's arm around him stopped his pacing and he dropped a kiss on her temple. He was well aware that she was highly worried about her brother and his now wife. Richard could only pray for the couple, knowing what they had faced. At least, he had been aware enough of what was happening when they had been forced to marry. To hear that Rori had not been had been distressing for them all.

"What do we do to help them, Richard?" Raleigh kept her voice soft, her eyes on her brother. "How do we do this?"

Richard shrugged, his heart raising in prayer for the couple.

"I don't know, love. I really don't." He peered into the sunroom, watching as Rori seemed to be sleeping, his arms wrapped around Brit and keeping her close to him. "I don't know what to say this time. He's hurting and so is she."

"They are." Raleigh moved away, heading for the kitchen where she could hear low voices. Becc and Bevan had refused to leave that night. They had returned with clothes and whatnot for Brit, knowing that she wasn't going to her own home either.

"Raleigh?" Becc moved to stand in front of the older lady, her arms wrapped around her self but restless movements of her feet showing her agitation and worry. "Why?"

"Why were they forced to marry?" Raleigh reached to hug Becc and then Bevan. "I don't know, Becc, Bevan. I really don't. Neither Rori or Britt seem to know either. But I do know that God is here and in control. He will protect them even if they or we don't like what they may still be facing. It's how He works. He will use His children to bring others to justice. We have seen that far too often with our friends." She gave a sad smile. "And it's not easy being the one going through this or to be the ones on the sidelines watching and praying. We pray for someone to stand in the gap for them. Sometimes, that happens. Quite often, it doesn't. We never know what God has saved or protected us from."

Bevan nodded, even as his gaze searched the room. He didn't take in the comfort that oozed from the colour choices or photos on the walls. Instead, he sought to understand what had happened and just could not.

Richard moved quietly to sit near his brother-in-law, studying the couple before his head dropped and his eyes closed. All he could do at present was pray for him.

An hour later, Richard's head raised as he heard a whimper. A frown crossed his face as he saw the agitation that had become evident in Brit. His hands were on the chair arm to push himself upright before he paused. Rori had simply gathered Brit closer to him as she moved restlessly, his eyes opening for a brief moment before he slept again.

Richard was on his feet, moving through his house and then around the outside of it. He stared towards his work buildings before he shook his head. He was not going that way, not at this time of night and not on his own. Someone was out there, just waiting for one of the family to head that way. His head turned as he felt someone approach him.

Bevan stared between Richard and the buildings. His voice was quiet as he spoke.

"Richard?"

Richard could hear the unspoken question in Bevan's voice before he reached out and turned Bevan back to the house. He walked into the kitchen, closing and locking the door behind him before he studied the younger man.

"Bevan? I thought that you were asleep."

"I was." Bevan rubbed at his face, fatigue drawing him down. "I'm glad tomorrow is Saturday and we don't have to work. We need this time." Bevan looked up at Richard, studying the other man. "What was going on out there?"

"Someone was near the buildings, just waiting for one of us to head that way. And I won't, not on my own. My team will be here tomorrow as will my friend, Don, and his team. We'll search. You and Becc need to be very careful as well."

Bevan nodded. He had gotten that message loud and clear as had Becc. He just didn't know how they would manage to do that.

"How do we do this, Richard? I never thought that any of us would be in danger, not like this." He looked around as he heard footsteps and Brit appeared beside him, her arm hugging her brother. "Brit?"

"It's okay, Bevan. We'll get there." She yawned. "Do you have coffee, Richard? My brain is not going to stop. I need to figure this out."

Richard gave a grin as Bevan simply turned his sister and walked her back to where Rori was still sleeping. He shook his head before he too yawned. He heard the sounds of Bevan's feet as he made his way back to the room that he was using for the night before he too headed for his bed.

Rori roused in the early morning hours, a hand rubbing at his cheek. He stared around, not really recognizing where he was for the moment. He squinted in the low light before his gaze landed on his hand. Rori frowned. Why was he wearing a wedding band? He hadn't been dating or even interested in a lady. He felt the heaviness on his shoulder and his head turned. Frowning even deeper, Rori stared at the lady who he was holding tight to him. His head tilted as he studied her and then sighed. Why was Brit here? And why was he holding on to her?

Brit stirred slightly as she felt Rori rising before she sank back into sleep. Her dreams were disturbing, she decided as she slept once more, not sure where she was or why. Those answers would come soon. What neither of the couple realized was just how dangerous it would get and that God would protect them in many ways, ways that they would not even be aware off. Rori whispered a prayer for them both as he walked away, not sure where he was heading but not wanting to leave Brit at all. His steps paused as he searched his sister's home, sensing evil approaching them and not aware of just how dangerous it would actually get for them.

Chapter 13

Brit was on her feet the next morning, walking away from the house and towards the road. She paused as she realized that she had no transportation and sighed, turning as she heard a vehicle stopping beside her. Timothy and Stephen, two of Richard's team, shared a look before they both studied Brit. She watched them in return, not sure of them and but knowing that they were indeed trustworthy.

"Can we give you a lift, Brit?" Stephen leaned forward to look around Timothy in the passenger's seat of his truck.

"You can. I need to go to my home and then to my building. Can you do that for me?"

Timothy was out of the truck, helping Brit into his seat before she had almost finished her words. He knew that Rori would be looking for her shortly. For now, he climbed into the back seat of the truck and nodded as Thomas looked back at him. A simple text message was sent off to Richard, who responded for the two men to stay with her.

Brit walked slowly through her home. It didn't seem the same to her any more and she was puzzled at that. She paused in her home office, her head dropping as she prayed. Only God would and could protect her. She had that amount of faith in Him. She might not like what she was going through but He had walked that path before her. Brit studied the ring on her finger, a puzzled look on her face. Just what was the reason for making them marry? And in such a rush? They hadn't been given an option, that much she could recall. Brit just wished that it had been different.

Her head turned as she heard footsteps stop in the doorway and looked at Stephen. He gave a gentle smile even as he prayed audibly for both Rori and herself. That seemed to relieve some of Brit's tension but not it all.

"Ready to go, Brit? There's no rush. We're free for the day. In fact, our wives would like to meet with you, if you're up to it." Stephen waited patiently for Brit to respond all the while assessing her.

Brit shrugged, not sure why they would want to do that. She stared out of the side window of the truck as Timothy drove towards her office and work space. She wasn't sure that she even wanted to be there but she needed to be. Brit had pending work that needed to be done and she couldn't do that if she remained in hiding.

"Does Rori know where you are?" Timothy's quiet voice sounded from the back seat.

"Not likely. We're not a couple, Timothy, even though it seems that way. We'll go our separate ways. I just wish that I knew why and who."

"It will come, Brit. It may take a while but we'll get it figured out. You're family now as are your siblings. We will not walk away from any of you." Timothy's voice was firm but Brit was shaking her head. "No, Brit, we will not walk away from any of you. I would suspect that Rori will track you down shortly."

"He shouldn't. He has his own life and work and he needs to look after that." Brit was out of the truck almost before Stephen had stopped, unlocking her office door and then shutting it and locking it after her. She needed to be alone and those two men just didn't seem as if that's what they would do.

Timothy and Stephen shared a look before they were both out of the truck, walking through the area and then studying Brit's office.

"She had to do that, didn't she?" Stephen was a little amazed at how quick she had moved.

"She did. Rori's going to have a time keeping track of her." Timothy sighed. "It's not like us or even Richard and Raleigh. Those two were a couple. Rori and Brit? They're not there yet. I don't know if they ever will be."

"You're correct, Timothy. I can see Brit walking away. Only, I don't know that Rori will let her." Stephen leaned against his truck, his arms crossing as he did so. "How do we help them? Brit is adamant, I think, that she wants to do it on her own."

"She will be. All our ladies were like that. How do we help? By praying for them. Being there when we can and they will allow us but also when they won't. Rori will fight us." Timothy sighed. "I just wish that he could remember what happened to him."

"I don't know that he ever will." Stephen looked around as he heard a car door shut and watched as Bill and Lily walked towards Brit's office. "I wonder if she'll let them in."

The two men watched as Bill hammered at the door when Brit did not respond at first. They could see her as she opened the door, argued with Bill, and then stepped back to let the two officers inside. They shrugged as they shared a glance before Timothy headed that way, his hand on the door knob that twisted under it. He stepped inside, hearing a raised voice from the work area. He shook his head. Brit was in fine form, he decided, not knowing if this was how she usually reacted.

Bill stood his ground in front of Brit. She was not cooperating with him, about what he had expected.

"I have to work, Bill, and I can't have anyone in the same room as I am. It just won't work." Brit was refusing to back down from Bill.

"We understand that, Brit. We need to place someone here with you, though, for the next few days. Richard has offered that as has friends of his who have security teams. It's not about just you. It's about Rori. We need to place someone with him as well once he's back to work. And with you two married, you'll be together after hours." Bill was frowning as Brit backed away from him, her head shaking. "Brit? That's happening."

"No, it's not. Now, if you have nothing further, I need to work." Brit pointed to the door, almost shoving them out. Her hand rested against it before her head turned. It didn't surprise her that Timothy was there. "Where's Stephen?"

"Outside." Timothy approached carefully, his head tilting to study her. "Bill's right, you know."

"About what?"

"About having someone with you. Today, that's Stephen and I. And then there's your free time."

"Go home, Timothy." The door opened once more under her hand. "Go home. And keep Rori away from me." She almost slammed the door after him, leaving him to stare back at it, Stephen appearing at his side.

"Didn't go well?" Stephen wasn't sure what to ask or even think.

"No, it didn't. Somehow, I don't think that she'll be with Rori. She's determined to keep herself safe. And only God can work on that." Timothy was frustrated, knowing that they had to keep both Rori and Britt safe. He just wasn't sure how they would do that.

Chapter 14

Facing his father across the desk in the main office, Rori swayed for a moment. He was not ready to work, not yet, but he was determined to. Ross studied his son, knowing that Rori would not be able to work for a while. He sighed to himself. This was coming into a busy time for them, with trade shows and craft shows approaching.

"Rori, you can't work. You're not steady enough to yet. Have you remembered anything?" Ross approached his son from around the desk and shoved him into a seat, taking with thanks the coffee that his secretary handed him. He prayed for his son, for healing and for understanding of what had happened.

"I haven't, Dad, and I need to. Brit is at risk for some reason. Do you know why?" Rori looked up, hope in his eyes even as he saw his father shaking his head.

"I don't know why, son. Bill has been around as has Jason and Lily. They're all working it but they don't have a lot of information to search through. They are praying that you remember what happened to you and who did this."

Rori's head dropped into his hands. Why, God? This had become his constant refrain over the last few hours. He lifted his head, sorrow on his face.

"Brit? Where is she?"

"Richard said that she was at her office. Apparently, Timothy and Stephen are with her." Ross gave a grim smile. "She kicked Bill and Lily out."

"She did? I don't think that would go over too well." Rori stared at his father as he continued to smile. "Dad?"

"It's okay, son. Timothy is in the building with her. He stays until she goes home." Ross hesitated to speak any further. What neither man knew was that Timothy had been locked out of the building as well.

"Will she come to me, Dad? Do you think that?" Rori wanted to run to find the lady who was his bride, but he had to wait. God was in control and would protect her, that much he knew. He also knew that he was in no shape to do that.

"I don't know, Rori. I really don't know. I don't know your lady. None of us do." Ross watched his son closely before his hand was out to draw him to his feet. "Come on, son. Mom's waiting to take you home. You need to rest and recover. And you're not going to do that here. We'll work around what we need to. We don't have to go to all the shows. In fact, I was intending on cutting back on them. The on-line store is taking off so well, we don't have to be out there now."

Rori nodded, his actions slow as he walked towards his mother. He hated this, he decided, unable to do anything much without being overly fatigued. He wanted the men who had done this to him but more than that, he wanted the men who had harmed Brit.

Brit turned late that afternoon from her kitchen counter. She could hear her siblings' voices as they entered her home. She had not reached out to Rori, choosing instead to be brought home. Brit had shut and locked the door before Timothy had a chance to enter, leaving him to drop his head down before he was walking around the house, just to assure himself that she was safe. Stephen had met him with a grin on his face before they were heading for Rori. Only, they didn't know what they would find when they found their friend.

"Brit? You're here?" Becc reached to hug her sister. "Where's Rori?" She frowned at her sister as Brit just shrugged.

"At home, I suspect. And no, I am not going there." She held up her hand. "I don't know if this is even legal, seeing it was under duress. I have my lawyer researching that."

"And if it isn't? What then?" Bevan reached for the coffee pot, intent on making that for them. "And you do need to eat, Brit."

"I know. There's some chicken we could grill." Brit's words stopped. "On second thought, just order something Bevan. I want the grill checked out before we use it."

"You don't think?" Becc's face paled even as she was unable to complete her sentence.

"I don't know, Becc, but I refuse to take any chances." She frowned towards where her phone lay on the counter. "That has been going off way too much." She picked it up, walking away from her siblings, leaving them staring after her and then at one another.

Brit ignored the doorbell, heading instead for her bedroom. She shut the door quietly behind her before she searched the room. It no longer seemed safe to her but she had no idea why. A tap at her door roused her from her thoughts before she turned to face Becc.

"Bill and Andrew are here, Brit. They want to talk to them." Becc frowned at her sister, not sure what was going on with her. "Brit? Why is this happening to you? And to Rori?"

Brit studied her younger sister before she reached to hug her, holding on tightly. Becc's tears fell for a moment before she sniffed, trying to control her emotions.

"I don't know why, Becc. I really and truly don't. I think it has something to do with my work, but I can't prove that. I'm not sure anyone can say why as yet. And if Rori doesn't or won't remember, then there's that." She looked down at her sister. "How do I keep you safe, Becc, you and Bevan?"

"It's not up to you, is it, Brit? You have always told us that God is the One in control. That He only wants the best for us. You said that God protects us even when we don't like what we have to face. We went through losing Mom and Dad together. Don't shut us out of this."

Brit hugged her sister tighter for a moment, her own tears near the surface before she began to pray, begging God for peace and safety and a soon ending to whatever it was she was involved in.

"I guess that I have to face those two, do I?" Brit gave a quick grin as Becc nodded and then stepped backwards. "I will not walk away from you or Bevan. We've been through too much to do that. As to Rori? I don't know what to say or even think. Until or unless he remembers what happened or who took him, we're at a standstill."

Brit stopped where she could watch both Bill and Andrew. She knew that they were friends with Richard, his team, and also Rori. She just didn't know how that friendship would affect her or their investigation.

Andrew turned as he sensed Brit nearby, assessing her. She's hurting, he decided, and it's no wonder. I need to get Phoebe here to speak with her. What we went through will help, I think, and so will the others who faced danger and conquered.

"Brit? Can we talk?" Andrew stepped towards her, finding apprehension on her face. "We do need to."

"I know. And I also know that you need to keep Rori away from me." She sighed at his smile and at how he shook his head. "He has to. Just so you know, my lawyer is investigating the marriage. It may not be legal if it was done under duress."

"It has been registered, Brit. I'm not sure where you go from here but I do know that Rori will not walk away from you or leave you on your own. Whether you want him around you or not, for now you two are married. And you do need to discuss that." Andrew would not let her away with walking from any of them.

Chapter 15

Brit shook her head, not hearing the door as it opened and closed again. Bevan followed Rori and Riley as they walked towards the kitchen, hesitating in the doorway as he watched his sister. Brit was not backing down from Andrew, not one inch, and she needed to listen. That was obvious that she wasn't prepared to hear what Andrew was saying and asking.

"Not happening, Andrew. For now, I am here. Rori needs to go on with his life." Brit heard a small sound of disagreement but didn't turn from watching Andrew. She saw his eyes flick to the side before they were back on her.

"It has to, Brit. Keeping you two together may be the only way to solve this as we keep you safe." Andrew nodded behind her. "Rori is here. You two need to talk and talk now." He walked away, shutting the door behind him. His head rested back on the steel door as he looked up, begging God to protect his friend and his lady. He just didn't know how that would happen.

Rori stood and watched his lady as he had become to think of her. He was frustrated at not remembering anything. For now, Brit was his lifeline to his past or the past that had just happened. He couldn't remember anything or was it that he refused to? Richard had asked him what had happened. All Rori could do was shrug. He had no idea what had transpired and he really did need to remember. His eyes rested on Bill for a moment before they moved back to Brit.

Walking around the table, Rori faced Brit, seeing the shuttered look on her face. This was not what was needed, he knew. They needed to talk but it was unlikely to happen any time soon. Bill had touched his shoulder as he left, a simply call me later uttered in a low voice. Riley had disappeared with Bevan and Becc, leaving the couple facing one another, not a couple per se, but two people whose lives had been joined by evil.

"Brit? We need to talk." Rori's hands grasped at the oak chair in front of him, not steady on his feet, but not willing to allow his fatigue and pain to send him away or even to a chair.

"There's nothing to talk about, Rori. I think we need to keep ourselves away from one another." Brit refused to back down, refused to acknowledge that Rori was beginning to creep into her heart and heal it. She knew that God was in control and had allowed what had transpired. She just didn't have to like it.

"We're married, Brit." Rori's words stopped as she vigorously shook her head. "We are, Brit. It's registered. Richard proved that."

"It may be registered and legal, but we both know that you were not even aware of what had happened or what you were forced to do. It was under duress. That makes a difference." Brit stepped towards the table, pulling the ring from her finger. It sounded harsh for a moment in the silent room as she dropped it in front of him. "Take that and please leave,

Rori. Don't contact me again." Brit walked away, not seeing the devastation that landed on Rori's face.

Rori stared after Brit, completely taken aback and then devastated that she walked away from him. He needed her. She was his lifeline, he thought. Rori stared down at the ring on the table before he picked it up. He frowned for a moment before he set the ring back down. Rori would not take it. He also would not walk away from his lady.

Riley hesitated as he stepped back into the kitchen, closing the back door behind him in a quiet manner. He frowned at the look on Rori's face and then searched the room for Brit.

"Where's Brit?" Riley's voice was quiet but still caused Rori to jump.

"I don't know. She's walked away from me, Riley. I don't want her to." Rori's finger rested on the gold ring laying on the teal tablecloth.

"Rori? What's this?" Riley stood beside his friend, a hand on his shoulder. "What did Brit do?"

"She's says that we're not married, that it's not legal. Please, God, I need her." Rori almost ran from the room, Riley staring after him before he was running after his friend.

Riley caught Rori as he collapsed beside his truck, lifting him up to the passenger seat and then running to climb behind the wheel. Riley stared at the house for a moment, knowing that Rori was hurting in a way that he had never seen someone hurt, not even himself and Rayleen or any of Richard's team or their friends. He shot a look at Rori, his white face scaring Riley before he headed for the hospital and care for his friend.

Richard paced the waiting room, his eyes on Raleigh. He was worried about his wife and their unborn child, knowing that she was fretting and more than a little worried about her brother. He didn't understand what had happened. Riley had not been clear with his words before he had taken off again, not saying where he was heading.

Riley hammered at Brit's door, not knowing if she was still there or if she would even answer. He waited and then hammered louder. He could hear the muttering as Brit approached the door. He prayed for Rori, not knowing if he was even still alive. The look on his face and his collapse had scared Riley.

"Riley?" Brit glared at him as she held the door in an almost closed position. "What are you doing here? You left."

"I did. Rori collapsed as he walked out of your house, no, make that ran. You need to be there." He reached for her hand, not letting her tug it away. "Stop this, Brit. You can run later. For now, please? Just be there for him?" Riley was begging, he knew, but he could do nothing else.

Brit stared at him in horror, not moving. She was unable to think clearly. Riley reached for her hand, trying to pull her from the house. She stepped backwards, the door opening more as he followed to stand just inside the door.

"I don't know what I can do, Riley. I'm not in his life, not any more. Not that I ever was, not really." Brit refused to move forward, her head shaking in the negative. She looked past him at that moment, a scream coming from her as men moved towards them.

Riley started to turn but was struck down before he had managed even a small turn. He sprawled face down on the floor. Brit stared at him in horror before her own wrist was grasped in a hard tight grip and pulled behind her back. She stared at the man who sauntered into her home, an arrogant sneer on his face.

Chapter 16

Brit stared at Riley in horror, not knowing if he was alive or dead. He had made no movement after he went down, and he had gone down hard. Her gaze returned to the man who now stood in front of her, a menacing look on his face. She tried to move away from him but the man's grip on her arm prevented that from happening. Brit whimpered with pain, twisting her wrist as best she could to try and escape. That just didn't happen.

The man in front of her stared at her in disdain before he looked down at Riley and then at the three men who surrounded him.

"You are coming with us, little lady." The disdain he had on his face sounded loud and clear in his voice. "You will work for me."

All Brit could do at that point was pray, begging God to release her and Riley and let them flee from this man. The evil that was emanating from him almost overwhelmed her, causing her to grow even more fearful for them both. Her head began to shake negatively in almost a violent manner.

"No, I'm not. I won't work for you." Brit knew the man, Edward Younge by name and reputation. He was notorious for running with criminals.

"Oh yes, you will. You and that man of yours." Younge stared at her and then the hand that was being held in the air. "Your ring? Where is it?"

Brit refused to speak, staring at him, blinking to control the tears of fear that welled in her eyes.

One of the men reached for the ring and handed it to Younge. He stared at it and then at Brit, reaching to forcefully shove the ring back on her finger.

"You don't remove it, ever!" He turned as he heard a slight noise, motioning two of his men to head back outside. He wasn't afraid, or so he claimed. But in the deep recesses of his black heart, he was terrified. Terrified that someone would catch up with him some day and repay him for his crimes. Younge frowned at Brit and then at Riley. He shook with rage for a moment before he heard the soft sound of a bullet fired from a silenced revolver. Whoever it was who had appeared had been dealt with. He now had to deal with Brit and that he could already tell would be a task in itself.

Brit was dragged from the house through the back door and then through her neighbour's yard until she reached the street behind her home. She fought all the while to escape, not able to free her wrist from the hard iron grip it was held in. Brit could hear Younge behind her, his complaints loud and clear that he had to come and find her. She would never escape from him again. Brit turned her head for a moment, prayers offered for Riley and then for whoever it was that had been shot. Her thoughts turned to Rori and then to her siblings. Fear rose within her as she prayed for their safety and begged God to protect them.

Jason Long had left his office in the police department about thirty minutes earlier. He was frustrated that they were no further ahead in their search for answers. To have Rori collapse again had not been what they had expected or wanted. He had talked long with Bill and Andrew and then headed out, not sure where to search any more. He prayed for his friends and for Brit and her siblings, knowing that God was the only one who could and would protect them fully. Not that they would like what they had to go through. He had faced that with his sister and her now husband.

Approaching Brit's home, Jason frowned at the open door. That wasn't expected. He slipped from his car, heading for the open door, not seeing the men who had appeared. As he looked up, Jason's forward walk stopped and he threw himself to one side. It just wasn't soon enough to draw his weapon or avoid the bullet that found his body. Landing heavily, Jason's head raised for a moment before it landed back on the soft green grass and his eyes closed as his consciousness faded. The men stood over him before they looked at each other, shrugged, and then turned to find Younge.

Bill was on a search through the department. Information had come in on another case that he and Jason were working and he needed to speak with him. He frowned. Jason was not there. Bill's face paled as he turned and ran for his car, speeding away towards Brit's home. He slammed on the brakes of his car and was out of it, running towards the body on the lawn. Bill's heart dropped as he realized that it was Jason, still alive, but injured. His phone out to call for help, Bill reached for his weapon and moved towards the home.

His eyes fell on Riley and once more his heart sank. They just didn't seem to be able to catch a break, he decided, as he determined that Riley was alive. He searched Brit's home, not finding her anywhere. He stopped at the kitchen table, eyeing it and not seeing the ring that had been placed there not that many hours previously.

Andrew stood nearby, having heard the call for assistance. He too looked around for Brit.

"No sigh of Brit?" Andrew waited somewhat impatiently for Bill to respond.

"No, there isn't. And the ring is gone." Bill was frustrated at the lack of evidence. He didn't think that Brit was hiding anywhere and he also didn't think that she would have walked away on her own and left the two men as they are. Bill searched the house. "There were other people here, Andrew. And I want to know who."

"Her security system?" Andrew searched for the control panel and pried open the cover, his gloved hands careful in his movements. "We'll need someone to look at it but I don't see that it has been tampered with." He was frustrated as well. He had an officer down, who was a friend, and also another friend down as well. He also had a friend in the hospital who was not rousing enough for them to speak with.

"I called Maria. Julia and Mark were there and would take her in. Faith and Josiah were there and will look after the little ones." Bill couldn't fathom how many friends, including himself and Andrew, had faced danger and their adventures when they meet their beloved mates.

"That's good. I'll head over there. Call in Lily. She was off tonight but we'll need her." Andrew walked away, his heart and steps heavy. He looked up for a moment at the darkening sky and just asked God why more friends were facing danger and death. He knew God was in control and had plans and purposes for them that they didn't know about. It just didn't help though to understand and know that, not in their humanness.

Chapter 17

Jason stared at Bill, his arm wrapped around his wife. He knew that his sister and her husband were standing nearby.

"What do you mean, Bill? Brit's missing?" Jason's left arm was in a sling, the bullet creasing the outer edge of his upper arm.

"Just that. Riley was down in the entry way and Brit was gone. It looks as if she was walked out of the back door." Bill turned as he heard footsteps and then excused himself. "Lily?"

"It's okay, Bill. I just needed to let you know that Riley is awake and gone. He's hurting that Brit disappeared on his watch as he put it. Richard let me know that Riley and Rayleen are with them as are their parents. Becc and Bevan have found them as well. Richard's team is drawing in on them as much as they can. Abe and Don have reached out as well." Lily named two other friends who had security teams.

"That's good. And that means Emma's involved. I don't know how she and her team manage to find the information that they do but it always helps to solve whatever it is." Bill rubbed at his face. He had planned on leaving when his shift ended and spending the evening with his wife, Cora, and his son and daughter. That was not happening.

"He didn't say much. He didn't see who it was. This is frustrating, Bill. How do we find Brit?" Lily turned to walk with Bill, who was heading for Rori's room on another floor.

"I don't know. She's a gemologist and I can see a criminal wanting to use her skills and knowledge that way. Rori? He's a glass blower. How would that be used in a criminal manner?" Bill was genuinely puzzled at Rori's disappearance as was everyone else.

Rori was sitting upright, his feet dangling just above the floor. He had dressed, despite the protest of his mother. He had stared her down and then asked her to leave. It was too dangerous, he had decided, for any lady to be near him. He didn't know that she had stopped just outside of his room door and bowed her head to pray for her son and his lady.

Bill hesitated for a moment, seeing Lily stopping beside Rebekah, an arm around the older lady. He walked towards Rori, seeing that Rori was finally alert and more like himself. Thank you, Lord, he whispered.

"Rori? How are you?" Bill stopped just short of the bed, patiently waiting for Rori to respond.

"How am I? I have no idea how I am to be. Do you?" Rori lifted his left hand. "And can you explain this? I'm not married. I'm not dating. Everyone knows that." His words were spit out at Bill, anger underlying them and also a touch of fear.

Bill sighed. Thanks, Lord, for letting me have to explain this to him.

"You are married, Rori. Not by your choice. You were taken captive twice. During the second captivity, Brit Morrison was with you. You were forced to marry. The marriage is registered but Brit is refusing to acknowledge it. She states that it wasn't legal as it was done under duress."

"Where is Brit? I want to speak with her." Rori slid to the floor, wavering for a moment until he found his balance. "Bill? What are you not saying?"

"Brit's been taken from her home. Riley was there and knocked out. He's fine and has gone to Richard's. Jason was winged by a bullet. The thing is that we don't know why or who." Bill was not backing down from his friend. "We need you to remember why you were taken and who took you first. The first time? Brit, Bevan, and Becc found you in a pit in the forest. And no, we don't know who dug that." Bill's words were like bullets firing at Rori. "We need to know what happened, Rori. To date, when you have been even a little bit lucid, you have not been able to tell us. And we have no idea why you keep collapsing. The physicians can't explain it."

"I don't know, Bill. I really don't know. How do we find out?" Rori walked past him, heading for the stairs and then down them.

Bill's head dropped for a moment before he was walking rapidly after Rori.

"Rori? Wait! You don't have any transportation. Come with me." Bill's hand on Rori's arm stopped his forward walk.

"I know that I don't, Bill. I want to find Brit. How do we do that?" Rori's face held a worried look even as he begged God to protect his lady. Without realizing how he was praying, Rori was accepting that Brit was his lady. He just had to ensure that she stayed safe.

"I don't know, Rori. In my car. Now!" Bill shoved Rori into the passenger side of his patrol vehicle before he was around it and then driving rapidly away, his eyes searching for those who were watching them.

"Bill?" Rori's vice held the question that he wouldn't ask.

"Someone was out there, Rori. You would have disappeared again, more than likely, and this time we may not have found you in time." Bill pulled to the side of the road and twisted in his seat to stare at Rori. "Where do I take you? You're going to be back at work. How safe is that?"

"We don't know, Bill. I can't remember what happened after I was at work. I don't remember Brit finding me. I don't remember being free and then taking captive again as you state happened. I don't remember marrying Brit. She deserves much better." Rori was almost in tears at thinking about Brit. "She deserves better than that." He paced the room before he looked over at Bill. "Take me home, Bill. I need to go there."

Bill shrugged. It was what he had expected Rori to say. He knew that Jason had gone home, Mark stopping by to tell him that.

"Okay, Rori. I take you home but you can't be on your own." Bill hesitated for a moment before Rori walked right by him and disappeared. Bill's head

90

dropped for a moment before he was searching for Rori and not finding him.

Rori turned to Richard and Raleigh, not surprised that they had appeared.

"I'm going home, guys. I need to do that." He was prepared for an argument from them.

"We know that you do, Rori." Raleigh twisted on her truck seat to study her beloved brother. "We've been through your home, Rori. I can't tell if anything has changed there."

Rori shrugged, not caring if any material possessions had disappeared or if something had appeared that would warn or harm him. His only thoughts were on Brit and where she was.

"Where's Brit?" His question didn't surprise them.

"We don't know, Rori." Richard grimaced, his thoughts dark as to what could have happened. "She disappeared from her home. And just so you know? The ring that she left on the table? It's gone as well."

Chapter 18

Rori wasn't surprised at that. Nothing was making sense, not one thing. He stared out at the passing streets and buildings, his thoughts troubled and dark. He began to pray, begging God to protect his lady. His prayer was sprinkled with God's promises of comfort, peace, and protection. Only God knew where his lady was and if she was still alive.

Rori drew in a deep breath as he sat on the side of his bed, a pair of heavy socks in his hand. He had showered, shaved, and then dressed in comfort clothes before he had found a seat. To say he was worried would be an understatement. He looked around as a tap came to his door.

Richard opened the door slightly and then stepped inside. He was exhausted as he knew that Raleigh was as well. She had found the spare room and stretched out, sound asleep within minutes. Neither one of them would walk away from Rori at that moment.

"Rori? What can we do for you?" Richard sat beside his brother-in-law, not sure what to ask or say. It had been different for him and Raleigh when they had been forced to marry. At least he remembered it.

Rori shrugged, deep fatigue hitting him hard. He blinked a few times.

"I don't know, Richard. I really don't know. Find Brit." His head turned to study the other man.

"Where are Becc and Bevan? This has to be so hard on them."

"It is. Your mom took them home with her for overnight. They both have work in the morning and need to be there." Richard stared ahead, not taking in the light teal walls and cream trim that Rori had chosen for his bedroom. "I don't understand, Rori. I just don't understand. Emma has been in touch but we haven't been able to tell her much at all. We don't even know if you were held here in town or somewhere else."

"I think it was in town, Richard. Don't ask me why. I think they dropped me into that pit. I can remember vague conversation but I wasn't alert enough to hear it very well or even understand what they were doing. I don't remember dropping down into that hole. I'm glad. It would be hard to live with."

"It would. Come with me, Rori. Raleigh has some soup ready for you. She's found a bed and is asleep." Richard stood, his hand out to steady Rori as he found his feet. He had managed to get the socks on his feet.

"That's good. This is disrupting everyone's lives. I want it over yesterday." Rori scowled at Richard as that man laughed.

"We all said that." Richard turned from dishing up the bowl of soup for Rori and then set it in front of him. "Eat, Rori. Then we pray."

Rori raised his head at last, feeling as if he had walked right into heaven and into God's presence. Richard's prayers always did that. And his usual closing of "I love You" only confirmed that Richard's love for and trust in God ranked first in his life.

"Tell me, Rori. Can a criminal use your glass blowing skills in any way?" Richard waited patiently for Rori to consider that.

"Not really. I mean, I am sure someone would figure out how to do that. We use glass, not any contraband." Rori frowned at Richard. "Now, if something was added to the packages, then they could. Smuggling is always a possibility."

"It is. Now, with Brit's occupation, I can see why they would want her. I just don't understand you. You didn't know her from before, did you?" Richard again waited patiently for Rori to consider his question and then respond.

Rori went to shake before his eyes closed.

"I did. We've been at conferences at the same time and ended up at the same table, side by side. We're also in the same Bible study at church. I don't know her very well other than to talk casually with her. Is that why? Is that why I was taken, to get her to cooperate?"

Richard stared at him before his head nodded.

"Silver had had that thought. She's in the same group as you two are. She has felt a sense of evil around you two the last week or so, but she couldn't pinpoint it to anyone. And that has bothered her so much. Silver was planning on speaking with you and then you disappeared." Richard rubbed at his cheek, fatigue weighing his body down.

"I see. You need to get some sleep, Richard." Rori was on his feet, clearing away his dishes before a hand rested on Richard's shoulder. "Thank you, Richard." He walked away, leaving Richard to stand and stare after him before his head dropped.

Ross turned to face his son the next morning. He shook his head. Rori should not be there. He wouldn't be doing any work for a while, that was obvious. It was also obvious that Rori was distracted by worry about his lady.

"Dad? Have you any word on Brit?" Rori paced his father's office, his hands clasped behind his neck.

"No, I haven't. And her parents haven't either. What is going on, Rori? You disappear, reappear, disappear and then reappear again, married to Brit. You collapse and she disappears."

"I know, Dad. I can't explain it. Richard asked if we were close or good friends. We're not or we weren't. We were in groups together and occasionally ate out with those groups. Somehow, she would end up sitting next to me. But it was hard to get to know her. She kept her personal life close to herself."

"She does. Bevan and Becc are the same but not to the same degree. Part of it is that she has had to raise those two. Other part is her work. She's a gemologist, correct?" Ross waited for his son to think that through and then nod. "Sit, Rori. You're going to fall over if you don't? He grinned at his son as Rori glared at him for a moment before he found the brown leather chair he favoured.

"She is. I'm not sure what all she does but it could be what they were after in the first place. Richard asked me if I thought that I was taken to put pressure on Brit, that somehow someone has decided that we're good friends or something more."

"That's a possibility. That doesn't explain you two being forced to marry." Ross leaned back in his black leather office chair, his eyes on the work and papers that were piled on his desk. He needed work through those but with the orders piling up and with Rori not able to work, he would be out in the work room. "Rori, I'll need you to pick up here in the office even if it's not what you want to do."

"I know, Dad. I can do that. At least part days for now. I'm just so tired."

"And you will be until whatever it is that was used on you is through your system. Did they ever determine just what it was?"

"No chemicals or drugs. That much we know. The physician thinks that whatever it was scared me so bad that I shut down. And I don't know what that would have been."

"Brit." Rori's eyes were on his mother as she sat beside him. Rebekah reached for his hand. "Brit is the constant in this, Rori. If they threatened her, you might have shut down. You care for her." Her hand went up as he went to respond. "Any lady in danger would be who you would want to protect. I have seen how you watch her, son, without you being aware. You have interest in her. I can't tell what her feelings are." Her head bowed as she began to pray for her son and his bride, knowing that God had walked the path before them and knew what He would allow to happen.

Chapter 19

Brit had fought her captor, trying her best to free her wrist, even to clawing at his hand. Nothing worked. Instead, she was just dragged down the street towards a building near her home and then into it, the door closing and locking behind her. One of the men planted himself in front of the windowless steel door, his eyes hard as he watched her, a hand on his weapon. Brit began to shake with fear, not knowing what was expected of her. She turned in fury towards Younge, finding him disappearing into an office.

Shoved down into a steel, armless chair, Brit struggled to rise but her captor's hands sat heavy on her shoulders, preventing her from moving. This was not what she wanted. She wanted to go back to her life as it had been a week ago and that didn't seem to be happening. Not sure what was happening, Brit stared at the steel work table in front of her. She grew more and more afraid. Tools of her trade of a gemologist sat there. What was he expecting her to do? There was no way that she would become involved in anything illegal and that seemed to be exactly what he was expecting.

Younge stood where he could watch Brit, anger on his face. He needed her to work for him. There were jewels that he needed her to manufacture and from the look on her face, she wouldn't willingly do that. He was under a time crunch from his employer. Using Rori against her didn't seem to have worked. Brit had walked away from him, totally unexpected.

Younge had fully expected her to stay with the younger man and not be found on her own. How to rectify what he was now finding would be a challenge, a challenge he was determined to win. Younge just didn't know the forces that were surrounding Brit and Rori and protecting them. God was there in the room. His angels were present. Younge would not be able to harm Brit to any extent without God allowing it. He also didn't understand that Brit could not manufacture the stones that he wanted. That was not what she did.

Brit grew still, her heart crying out to God and begging for release. Then, her prayers changed to begging for peace and safety in her situation. She had no idea what Younge had planned but it was something that she would not be a part of. Brit knew that Younge was behind her somewhere, watching and assessing her. Her face became a blank canvas as she shuttered her emotions and fear deep within her. He would not win, not that way.

"Well, little lady, you're going to work for me." Younge paced towards her, his footsteps heavy on the floor. "We have what you need for you to manufacture jewels."

Brit shook her head. Obviously, he had no idea of what her work actually entailed.

"I can't do that. I don't make jewels. That's done in a laboratory and I am not that person." Her tongue came out to touch the blood on her lip. Younge had not taken her words very well and a blow to the face had followed, his anger palpable in the room. "Was that really necessary? I don't make jewels. Go look up the definition of a gemologist and you'll see that." Her eyes were steady on his, causing him to frown. Brit was not acting as anyone whom he had in his custody usually did. He backed away from her and then left the room, nodding at his men to follow.

Younge paced his office, frustrated at her words. He had turned to his phone, frowning at the messages that he was receiving from his employer. They were getting angry with him and also frustrated at how long it was taken to force Brit to work for them. It hadn't worked taking Rori captive. He had shut down the first day from the threats. Even dropping him into the pit that day and having Brit and her siblings rescue him had not worked. Their forced marriage was another problem that he needed to solve. That had not worked out as he had planned. Brit just had not stayed with Rori. Younge had heard rumours that she was investigating the legality of the marriage. That had to stop.

The younger man employed by Younge stood in the hallway where he could see into the office and also the room where Brit was locked into. He shook his head. He had not expected to become party to violence, assaults, or kidnapping. He looked around and then paced away, heading for the small room that was his. He needed to think this through, he decided, and determine if there was any way that he could help Brit escape. When that happened, he would be with her and go to the authorities. From what he had been told, this was not the first time Younge had done something like this and he wanted to prevent it from happening again.

Brit sat quietly for the first hour or so after Younge had walked away. She knew that he would be back at some point and she didn't want to be caught unawares. Finally, she sighed and rose, walking around the table and peering at the tools there. He had done some research, she decided, but these tools were not what made jewels. And Brit would have no part of whatever it was that he had determined that she would partake in.

Her attention turned to the windows and she crossed to them. Peering outside, she noted that they were close to a forest and that twilight was descending. Glancing over her shoulder at the door, Brit reached for one of the windows. It rose under her hands. Brit shook her head. Younge certainly didn't think of what a person in captivity would try. She was out of the window, her feet landing on the soft grass below it before she jumped to lower the window.

Running for the trees, Brit shot a quick glance over her shoulder and nodded. So far, so good, she thought. She ran towards her home and then stopped. That would be the first place that they would look for her, she knew. Where could she go? Brit felt her pocket and shook her head. She still had her phone. No one had searched her, for which she was thankful. Her phone in her hand, she stared around, trying to decide who to call. Lily won the toss as she said.

"Lily?" Brit could hear activity in the background.

"Brit? Where are you?" Lily was on her feet, moving from her office and towards Bill. A hand on his arm stopped him in his tracks.

"I'm in the forest behind the high school. Can you come and get me?" Brit moved further into the trees, seeking somewhere that she could hide. "I've managed to get away but I don't know how soon he'll find that I've escaped."

Lily pulled Bill with her, despite his protests and questions.

"It's Brit. She has somehow escaped." Lily shot a look at Bill who was staring at her in shock. "She's near the high school." Her words stopped. "Younge."

"Younge? As in Edward Younge? He has a home near there, doesn't he?" Bill was on the phone to one of the other detectives, quickly asking for their aid in researching Younge. "That makes bizarre sense, you know. The rumours have always been there that he's into crime."

"They have been." Lily slowed her car as she approached the trees. "I just don't know where she'll be." Her phone was out as she sent a quick text to Brit, watching carefully. Neither she nor Bill saw the dark figure approaching until the back door of the car opened and Brit slipped inside. Lily drove away, not seeing anyone approaching them. Questions could and would wait until they had Brit safe at the department.

Younge stood in the room that had been locked, his hand on the light switch. Brit was nowhere to be found. How did that happen? He thundered through the house, his feet heavy as he tramped through the rooms, searching for whoever it was that had helped Brit to escape. They would pay and pay dearly.

Chapter 20

Brit rubbed at her wet hair, a thick towel in her hands. She felt dirty and unclean just from the contact with Younge. Even the hot shower, as hot as she could stand, didn't seem to relieve that feeling. She sighed to herself. This was not how her life was to be. Brit had plans and those plans did not include Rori or his family.

Walking through her home, Brit tilted her head. She breathed a sigh of relief. She had locked up after everyone, including her siblings, sending them all home. Brit needed to be on her own. She stared down at the ring that had been so roughly shoved back onto her finger. Fear flowed through her as she gazed at it before she was tearing it from her finger, a sob rising within her. She dropped it onto the kitchen counter, watching as it spun in a circle of golden reflected light, the metallic sound harsh in her ears. Brit didn't want to marry, didn't want to be responsible for someone else. She had had enough of that, she decided. Hearing her phone chime, Brit froze before she reached to wake it up, signing in with her passcode. She sighed. Of course, it would be Rori, reaching out to her. She had to decide how to avoid him and didn't know it that was at all possible.

Brit walked away from her kitchen, lights turned out as she headed for her office. She found a blanket to wrap around herself as she huddled down on the loveseat. She was too afraid to sleep but too tired to stay awake. She began to pray, knowing that God was in control and that He would protect her. Brit just didn't see that happening at all. This is where faith and trust in someone unseen came in, she knew. She had had that experience all too often over the years. Brit felt betrayed by those around her and for her to feel that meant that she withdrew into herself. It was how she coped.

Rori watched his phone, waiting for a reply from Brit before he sighed and set his phone to one side. Obviously, she was not ready or even willing to contact him. He knew that she was home and safe. Richard had been around to assure him of that after speaking with Bill. To have her avoid him was not what Rori wanted. He would track her down the next day, he decided, and force her to confront the elephant in the room so to say and decide what she wanted. He had spoken with both his lawyer and hers. Even under duress, their marriage was legal. Brit needed to hear that from him and to hear that he was not walking away from her. His eyes rose to the living room ceiling as he begged God for a chance with the lady he had decided that he loved. He prayed for protection for her and for himself and their families. He had no idea what was in store but his faith and trust was in the One who did, who had walked this very path before them and knew exactly what they were facing.

Rousing in the early morning hours, Brit sat upright on the loveseat, the blanket pulled tight around herself. She blinked, not sure what to think or even feel. A sound from outside of the house had her jumping, fear evident on her face. Brit was on her feet, tracking the sound as it moved around her home. She stood for a moment near the front door, peering through the window and sighed. Of course, there would be men out there. Isn't that what they always did? She could feel God's presence between herself and the door and knew that He had placed an angel there. She had felt that before.

The men withdrew from the house, not able to find a way in. That had frustrated them. They were under orders to find Brit and return her to their employer. There just didn't seem to be a way to do that.

Brit slumped back against the wall behind her, her head dropping. The men had left but by no means was she safe. Bill and Lily had emphasized that only too well. She had no idea where she could go to find safety. Her worry was that Becc and Bevan would be hurt in the man's attempt to force her to work for him. Brit frowned down at her ring, a though puzzling her. She pulled it from her finger once more and studied it. There was no way that she was putting it back on. Her lawyer had sent an email the night before that had stunned her and then saddened her. Rori had been correct. Their marriage was legal. Brit just didn't want that. She wanted her life back as it had been, just her siblings, herself, and her work. That seemed to no longer be the case.

Rori stood outside of Brit's home early that morning. The sun had arisen, promising a beautiful warm day. He just didn't see that. His whole attention was on the door that he had knocked at and that hadn't yet opened. Rori had confirmation that Brit was there. Becc stood beside him for a moment before she shook her head, a soft smile on her face.

"She's not going to open the door to you, you do know that?" Becc grinned at Rori as he stared at her in shock. "She won't. It's how she copes at times. She hides. Only this time? She can't be hiding. This affects more than just her or even Bevan and myself."

Unlocking the door, Becc shoved it open, not surprised to find her sister standing there and watching her, a frown on her face. Becc reached to hug her, holding on just a little bit tighter, a prayer whispered in Brit's ear. She knew that Bevan was behind her, waiting almost impatiently for his turn to hug his sister before he moved past her, heading for the kitchen. His voice was low as he spoke with Becc, both of them shooting glances back towards Brit and Rori.

Rori stepped inside, the door closing behind him as his hand fumbled for the deadbolt to set it. His eyes never moved from the lady who was his sweetheart.

"Rori? What are you doing here?" Brit's voice was weary and had a tone of almost anger in it. She didn't want to see Rori, didn't want to hear what he had to say.

"I had to come, Brit. I had to see that you were all right." Rori stepped towards her, his hands resting on her shoulders, feeling the tension that they held.

"You shouldn't be here. You need to be resting to recover." Brit's eyes never left Rori's, seeing something in there that cracked at the tight wall that she had around her heart. Rori was slowly but surely chipping away at it, freeing her to love and live as God would have her.

"I needed to see you, Brit sweetheart. We need to talk and talk today. Ignoring me or running away from me won't work. They have proven that, haven't they?" Rori's voice held a bite to it, startling Brit who was unable to move away from the tall handsome man standing in front of her as his hands tightened on her shoulders.

"What's to talk about, Rori? I want an annulment and my lawyer will be working on that." She frowned as Rori shook his head. "What?"

"I don't, Brit. I really and truly don't want that. For now? We need to stay together. They'll go after one or the other of us to get to us. And I for one want to know why." Rori began to pray for Brit and himself in a way that he had never done before.

Brit shook her head, not willing to fight him to walk away. And that both surprised and frightened her. She couldn't do that to him. Would she ever be able to walk away from him? She felt as if God was not allowing her to do that, that He wanted them together for a reason, a reason that Brit really wanted to know.

Chapter 21

Rori's gaze shifted to where he could see Bevan, who stood in the kitchen doorway, concern on his face before he shook his head and turned away. Rori sighed to himself. This was not going as he had planned or prayed for. He had forgotten that Brit was an individual with her own wishes, wants, dreams, and desires. Rori might never be part of that and that saddened him.

"Brit? Where can we talk? Or do you want to talk in front of Becc and Bevan? This is a conversation that we will have and have today."

Brit shoved at Rori's, her hands flat on his chest. He moved backwards, his hands dropping to his sides where they clenched and unclenched.

"There is nothing to say, Rori. Absolutely nothing. Don't even think that we are a couple. We're not and never will be. Whoever it is that is doing this? We'll find them, have them arrested, and then go on with our separate lives." Brit turned and walked away from him, ignoring his soft calls of her name and for her to wait. She didn't want him to see the tears streaming down her face, tears of fear and uncertainty and yes, of the wishes of a young lady searching for her soulmate.

Becc watched her sister walk away before she followed her. She knew Brit would react strongly to that but it was just too bad, she decided. This, whatever this was, was affecting all of them. Brit was too focused on what she wanted and had been for a few months, Becc realized.

"Brit?" Becc sat beside her sister, shoulders touching, waiting patiently for Brit to respond.

"What?" Brit bit at her lip. "I'm sorry, Becc. This has been going on for months, you know. I have felt someone watching and following me. I know that someone tried to access my building and couldn't."

"Did you tell anyone?"

Brit shook her head.

"No, there was no point. They can't see who was on the security system. They were that well disguised. And they can't investigate someone that they can't see." Brit shifted on the bed, her eyes on the door. "And now there's Rori."

"There's Rori. You can't run and hide from him, Brit. You need to face him. I know that you don't want to." Becc's hand went up as Brit's mouth opened to protest. "For now, and for all intents and purposes, you are a married couple. It may not be what you want, but God has allowed it. He has plans and purposes for us that we don't always see or understand. This is one of yours. Don't forget that He walked this path before you two and is there every step of the way. Talk to Rori. That's all he's asking for now. He's not asking you to move into his house or for him to move in here. That may never happen." Becc bit at her lip, not sure how to continue. She knew that Brit was watching her closely, waiting for her to finish. "I've watched Rori. He cares for you, Brit. He's watching you in the same way that Dad watched Mom. He's in love with you, sis, whether you want to accept that or not." Becc hugged her sister and then walked away, leaving Brit staring after her.

Rori waited somewhat impatiently for Brit to return, hope on his face that they would stay together. After about thirty minutes of just standing in her entryway, Rori turned, his shoulders slumping in defeat. This was not how he prayed the day would go. He found a seat on the stairs to her front porch and sat, not willing to walk away but not willing to stay. God was not letting him leave as yet. Raising his eyes, Rori searched the area. He could feel the eyes watching him and watching Brit's home. He was afraid for her, afraid that he would lose her before their life together had even started.

Bevan approached from the sidewalk, a cup of takeout coffee extended to Rori. Rori took it with a word of thanks and just held it, his eyes not moving from the house across the street.

Bevan found his seat beside Rori, not speaking, just being there if Rori wanted to talk. He knew it would take time for Brit to respond, if she did. Becc had simply shrugged when she found him, not sure what to say.

"That house across the street?" Rori finally spoke, his hand holding the cup of coffee raised to point at it. "Is it occupied?"

Bevan shook his head, a frown on his face.

"It hasn't been for a few years now. The old fellow passed away and it can't be sold yet. Or even rented from what we hear. Why?" Bevan shifted his gaze between Rori and the house.

"Because someone is living there. The signs are subtle but someone is watching us from there. Who would be doing that?" Rori sighed, knowing that he couldn't approach the house. He would need to reach out to Bill or Jason or even Lily.

"There is? I wonder if that's what Brit meant." Bevan shifted to stare back at the front door, not seeing anything through the window on it.

"What do you mean?" Rori finally looked at Bevan, seeing the struggle and stress that he was going through.

"She's mentioned feeling watched the last few months. She hasn't spoken to anyone. As she put it, they can't investigate feelings. And I don't know if she had directed her attention to that house." Bevan heard the door open quietly behind them. "Brit?"

"Is that where they are?" Brit sat between the two men who had shifted over to let her. Becc had left, having a commitment to get to that she really didn't want to go to.

"It's possible." Bevan handed his sister her own cup of coffee. "Drink it while it's hot this time, sis. You drink enough cold coffee as it is." He grinned as she made a face at him. He then shared a look over the top of her head with Rori, a look that said both men were committed to protecting the lady that they both loved.

"I see." She sipped at her coffee, a frown in place on her face. "God is here, guys. I know that He is. He's protecting us even though it doesn't feel like it. How do we go forward? And what have Bill and his fellow detectives discovered that they're not sharing with us?"

Chapter 22

Andrew McBeth, Elmton police chief, hesitated as he drew his personal vehicle to a stop in front on Brit's home. He knew that his officers and detectives were working on a search warrant for the house across the road, the family horrified that it might be used in a crime. He searched the area around him out of habit before he closed his car door and walked up the sidewalk, his eyes on Brit and Rori. Andrew frowned. They were still sitting side by side on the front steps, shoulders and legs touching. Even after Bevan had arisen and left, neither had moved, needing that contact with the other.

Rori squinted against the rays of sun before he shook his head. Andrew was here. That wasn't good, he decided.

"Andrew? You're here?" Rori studied Brit's face as Andrew took a seat beside her, seeing it was shuttered and closed.

"I am, Rori. Just as a friend. I'm off today. So, when I heard that you were both here, God sent me this way." He grinned at Rori before he too studied Brit. "Just how are you two doing?"

Rori shrugged, not sure how to respond. He knew the story of Andrew and his Phoebe, how they had faced danger and how God had protected them. He didn't know if Brit was aware of that.

"Okay, I guess. I see activity across the street." Rori nodded that way, setting his empty coffee cup to one side as he did so. He could hear the low voices from the officers mingling with the sounds of nature.

"There is. I'm not here because of that. That investigation is in good hands." Andrew studied the activity before he turned to Brit. "Brit? What can we do for you?"

Brit stared at him in shock for a moment. No one had asked her that, not yet. She frowned at him before she shrugged.

"Let me go back in time, Andrew, to before this all happened. And I know that is not possible. Rori needs to get on with his life and can't do that, not until this is solved." Brit was on her feet, walking down the sidewalk and then pacing away from the two men. Rori had risen and stepped down to the sidewalk, his eyes on her.

"She just walked away, Andrew. How safe is she?" Rori turned to his friend, seeing the compassionate look on Andrew's face.

"She'll be fine. Lily is waiting for her." Andrew nodded towards where Lily had stopped Brit. "She'll stay with her for now." He sighed. "But what about you?"

"Richard is threatening to stick me away somewhere. That's not happening." Rori gave a quick grin as Andrew laughed. "I'm back at work next week. I'm not sure how that will work out. Dad needs me there."

"And you are worried about Brit and how she'll survive." Andrew's hand was raised as Rori opened his mouth. He studied the area around Brit's house, liking that there was nothing in the garden that someone could hide behind. "She's running, Rori, just as we discussed. She's not ready to give in and accept the fact that you two are married and in it for the long haul."

"I know." Rori rubbed at his hair, not caring that he mussed it badly. "I don't want her to, Andrew. I can see us together for the rest of our lives, God willing. I just don't know if she will ever agree to that."

"It's hard loving them, Rori. I know that you've likely been talking to whoever it is that you can. You know the stories of Richard and his team and our friends as well as those of Bill, Lily, and myself." Andrew hesitated. "You also know the story of Silas and Madigan. Have you spoken with him?"

Rori nodded. Silas had reached out to him the day before and met with him as his pastor and also a friend. He needed that support. He just prayed for it all to be over so that he and Brit could discuss what and where they wanted to be.

Lily tucked Brit into her patrol car, her senses alert to danger approaching them. She couldn't see anyone but someone was out there. She had felt that danger when she and Loch had had their adventure as it was termed. She prayed for her new friend, not wanting Brit to go through what they had.

"Brit?" Lily slipped behind the wheel of her car and turned to Brit. "Where were you heading?"

Brit shrugged, not sure what to say. She had needed to walk away from Rori and Andrew, sensing that Rori wanted to talk with her about their marriage. She wasn't ready for that and didn't know if she ever would be. She could also sense the evil and danger approaching her and wanted to run as far as she could, praying that whoever it was would be left in the dust of her race from danger. Brit knew that she couldn't do that, that God was protecting them. She couldn't walk away from Bevan and Becc, not knowing if whoever it was would go after them.

"I don't know, Lily. I truly don't know. I just needed to get away from Rori. And Andrew showing up? He said as a friend but he's still a police officer. I can't see how he can separate the two."

"Andrew is able to do that very well, just as we can. He was there as a friend only, worried about you and Rori. For Andrew to be worried means that he takes steps, even if it is just to show up and pray for you." Lily turned to look behind her. "Come on. I'm off duty now. Jason will catch up with us later. For now, let's head to my home. Loch is away for the day. He's my sweetheart and husband and yes, we did have an adventure." She laughed at the look on Brit's face.

"What is it with you all? All of you?" Brit was astounded at that thought.

"All of us, and many other friends from Oak City and Riverville. Too many we think. But now, you need to forget about this for a while. How be we find a movie and some junk food? I hear tell that it works well to dull the danger around you." Lily was laughing as Brit sputtered out something that was not able to be understood.

Rori finally walked away from Brit's home, realizing that she was not returning at all that day. He needed to walk away, he decided, and let her have time to absorb the news. Only, he didn't think that they would have that much time.

Chapter 23

A week later, Rori walked through his work place, seeing the changes that his father was implementing. He had agreed with his father that their online store should become their focus. He just wasn't sure if this was the right time or not. Rori looked up as he neared the showroom, a frown on his face as he saw Brit standing there in front of him, shuffling from foot to foot in unease.

"Brit?" Rori reached to hug her, finding her responding to some degree before he released her and then reached for her hand, tugging her towards the office. "What are you doing here?" He shoved her into a chair and then sat beside her, moving his own chair as close to hers as he could.

Brit shrugged. She was not sure why she was there other than for the threat that she had found on her door over the lunch hour. Whoever it was that was stalking them knew that Brit and Rori were leading separate lives. She stared down at the paper before she thrust it at him.

"Read this." Brit could barely get out those two words.

"What is this? And where did it come from?" Rori held the paper, not looking at it. Instead, he kept his eyes on her.

"Read it." Brit folded her arms around herself, seeing Ross as he stopped behind his desk and then sat, nodding that he should stay.

Rori studied her closer before his eyes dropped to the paper. He drew in a deep breath. The wording was brutal, clearly stating that Rori and Brit needed to be in the same house from now on or one of them would either die or disappear.

"They said this?" Rori turned as Ross rose and approached his son, taking the paper from him. "Dad?"

Ross read the letter and then set it aside, his eyes on Brit. She's brittle, he decided, and almost ready to crack or run. That can't help with her work.

"Brit? Talk to us. Tell us exactly what you do." Ross found a seat where he could watch both of the younger people.

"What do I do? I'm a gemologist. There are different types of gemologists. For me, I assess the value of a gem and decide if it is genuine or not. That involves a lot of training. I have to keep updated all the time. If someone wanted me to falsify a report and say a gem is genuine when it's not, that's what they would be after me for although a jeweller could do that. I also have to testify in court as an expert witness at times. That I hate doing." Brit frowned at Ross. "Why do you ask that?"

"I knew that you were a gemologist. I just didn't know what role you had with the gems. Now, Rori here? He's my top glass blower. His creations are all over the world by now. I don't see how your gem knowledge ties in with his skills." Ross and Rori had discussed that in great detail.

"Richard asked the same thing, Dad." Rori sat back further in his chair. "We are at a loss, not knowing why we were forced to marry. I wish that I could remember what happened to start this all off."

"And you may never." Brit rubbed at her face before she hid it in her hands. "I don't get why you were taken."

Ross nodded. He could see the interest between the two in each other. A though crossed his mind.

"You have been connected in that person's mind for some reason. It may simply just have been a meal out with your group or sitting beside each other at some function. Whoever it is has connected you two. Rori, you have been kidnapped to start all this off to try and force Brit to come to terms. Only that didn't work out. Brit, during the days leading up to when you found Rori, did anything unusual happen to you or your brother or sister?"

Brit frowned at him as she thought that through before she shook her head.

"Not that I know of. The only unusual thing was finding that hole in the ground and Rori down in it. I still haven't figured out how they managed to dig that hole without anyone knowing about it."

"If they did it at night, no one would know. It's a fairly isolated place." Rori rose and began to pace. I still don't understand." He slipped back into his chair, a hand reaching for Brit. "Brit? Who chose the rings?"

"They did and I hate them." Brit stared at her ring, a horrible thought coming to her. "Has something been put into them, something that could track us?"

"That's possible. I would suggest that you change the rings, Rori, and turn those ones over to Bill." Ross rose, his eyes on the clock. "It's time to clock off, Rori. How be you take your lady out for a meal? Show them that you are a couple, at least for now. It may mean that you move into one of your houses for the time being." His hand went up at Brit's protest. "Just for now, Brit, until we can solve this."

Brit shook her head, walking away from the two men before Rori ran after her and with a hand on her arm, stopped her in her tracks. She refused to look at him, devastation evident on her face. Ross' words were not what she wanted to hear.

"Brit? We need to do this. He's not winning by us moving in together. We're doing that to flush him out. Richard would like to meet with us. I know that he's reached out to you. Please?" Rori knew that he was begging, but this was the love of his life, he had finally acknowledged, who was being threatened.

Brit finally gave an abrupt nod. She hated giving control of her life to anyone, even on a temporary basis. She had had to be strong for her siblings for too many years. Tears suddenly overwhelmed her as she listened to the late evening sounds. Having Rori wrap her into his arms had not been expected. She resisted for a moment, finding that he just refused to let her go. Brit relaxed against him, feeling safe for once.

"When?" Brit's voice was barely audible.

"Now, if you have the time." Rori walked her to her car, shutting the door after her before he ran for his truck, afraid that she would just take off and he would not be able to find her.

Ross stood in the doorway of his shop, watching the young couple, his heart torn with fear and worry. This was not over, he decided, not with the letter that Brit received. They needed to find out who and he had no idea how to do just that.

Chapter 24

Richard watched Raleigh closely as she stood talking with her brother. Rori had appeared, almost dragging Brit with him. He could see the reluctance of Brit to be there but he also saw the acceptance that she had to be.

"Brit?" Richard stopped beside her and then with a hand on her arm, drew her into his office, seating her and then finding his own chair. "Talk to me. What changed today? Rori has been keeping us updated as much as he can from what he's facing. But you? You haven't. Talk to me."

Brit stared around the room, taking in the comfortable atmosphere in it. She refused to look at Richard, knowing that when she did, her life would like change. It startled her as she began to hear him pray, specifically for her, ending his prayer with his usual "I love You". Brit turned to study him, finding him just sitting there, seemingly relaxed with his head still bowed.

Richard looked up at last, a peace radiating from him that Brit desperately wanted herself. How did he do this, she questioned before her own heart was raising in prayer, begging God for that very peace.

"Richard? What do you want to know?" Brit broke the silence in the room, her voice barely audible.

"What do I want to know? What did you receive today? Rori didn't bring you here just to see us. He and you need our help." Richard reached for the pad of paper and pen that sat beside him.

"A letter on my work door. It said that we had to start living together." Brit stared at the floor, embarrassed at having to admit that. "How do they know?"

"They are watching you that close." Richard frowned. "Your rings? Who chose them?"

"Not me. I would have refused to do that. And Rori wasn't aware enough to do that." Brit stared at him in horror before she was tearing the ring from her finger. "What's in it?"

"I don't know that anything is. Let me have yours and I'll get Rori's. Bill will take them to their lab and have them assess them." Richard sighed. It wasn't going to be easy to convince Brit that she and Rori needed to be together, even in the short term. He had watched Rori and knew that the younger man was in love with Brit. Brit, now? He couldn't read her.

Brit was on her feet, pacing, a troubled look on her face. She finally spun to face Richard, seeing that Rori and Raleigh were now seated in the room. She frowned at them before looking back at Richard.

"Is there any guarantee even if we were to live in the same house that this is over? Who is doing this? And what do they want?" Brit slumped back into her chair, defeated.

"We don't know yet, Brit." Richard reached for his phone that had been vibrating. He read his text and then grinned. "We have help on the way, Brit. Rori,

Emma's weighing in. She and Abe want to meet with you two tomorrow night, if they can."

"Who are they?" Brit wasn't ready to meet with anyone else, that much was clear in her mind.

"Abe has a security team, just as I do. Emma has a firm where she finds people, places, and information that no one else can. I didn't reach out to her. Somehow, she always seems to know when someone needs her help. And this time, it's you two." Richard's hand went up to stop Brit's words, seeing Rori nodding. "And there is no cost to you, Brit. They never charge friends."

Brit shrugged, not at all certain why Richard was saying that. He had a security team. Why would she need to know about Abe's?

Rori sat next to her, a troubled look on his face. He had started to receive those messages that hadn't been coming, the messages that threatened but vaguely. He had passed them on to whoever it was that needed them.

"Richard? Emma's involved?" Rori knew that was likely the case.

"She is. She wants to meet with you two sometime in the next few days. For now, what do we do with you two? Given that message? They will be looking for you to be together in one of your homes. It's not going to matter which one."

"No, it won't." Rori sighed, rubbing at his cheek, something he felt he had been doing too much off. He studied Richard, knowing that Richard was hurting for the couple.

"So, what do we do?" Brit was not backing down from either of the men. When they didn't answer, she was on her feet, almost running from the room, her phone out to call for a taxi. Before they could react, she was gone, heading for her home and what she prayed was safety. Only that didn't happen. Brit stared in horror at the broken down door to her home, seeing the police officers and crime scene techs moving around her property.

Bill walked towards Brit where she had dropped to the lawn across the street from her home. He could see the devastation on her face and in her bearing. He shook his head. Nothing seemed to have been taken or disturbed. Just the door broken down. Bill had made a call to a friend who was a carpenter and who promised to be there to replace the door. He stood for a moment staring down at Brit, not sure how to read her.

Brit looked up at Bill, one eye closed against the setting sun. She rose to her feet, uncertainty on her face.

"Brit? Where were you just now?" Bill's question caught her off guard.

"At Richard's with Rori. Why?" Brit stared past him at her home.

"They were looking for you, whoever they are. How do we keep you safe? And that letter? Are you going to do what they demand?" Bill had to ask.

"No, I'm not. I am not moving in with Rori or having him move in with me. That's not happening. We're not a couple, not matter what anyone else thinks." Brit had that tiny bit of spark of hope in her heart, that just maybe Rori would stay around and that they would grow to love one another. She could see the attraction that he had for her and was fighting to tamp down hers for him. This didn't happen in real life, she had decided. Couples didn't go into danger and then fall in love.

"That's what they were looking for, you know. To see if you had moved out or if he had moved in." Bill hesitated, not sure how to word what he needed to say. "It's going to come to that, Brit. At some point, we will have to put the two of you together. For now, Adam, a friend of ours, is on his way to fix your door. Your insurance agent?"

"I called him. He said to take photos and send them to him. He's out of town today." Brit sighed. "This is not what I wanted to find. I'm tired, Bill, and this is not helping." She walked away from him, leaving him to stare after her as he tucked away his pen and pad of paper.

Chapter 25

Rori looked up from where he was working on a glass vase and nodded at Bill. He was almost done for the day and needed to complete that glass work before he left. He was troubled about Brit, not having been able to contact her over the day. She seemed to be avoiding him and that just wasn't what was needed. Bill had called him the night before, just asking where the couple stood as a couple. He was not surprised to hear that they were questioning the rings and had sent a crime scene tech to Rori's to retrieve them.

Walking away at last from his work, Rori wiped at his brow. He was hot and exhausted. Bill following him towards their break room, shaking his head at the bottle of water Rori held up.

"Talk to me, Rori. What is going on now?" Bill had no idea where Rori was at present in his thoughts. That man was not sharing and he needed to.

"I really don't know, Bill. I can't reach Brit. She's not answering my calls or the text messages that I sent her. I'm planning on heading that way to speak with her." Rori frowned at Bill. "What can you tell me about where the investigation stands?"

"Not where we would like it. We have no evidence or confirmation of who is after you two or even why. We suspect it's Brit and her occupation. How would you work be used in crime?" Bill was puzzled by that, his discussion with Andrew not fruitful.

"How could it be used? The only way would be to put something into our shipments and we are very careful to watch for that. It has been a concern for a while." Rori leaned against the counter, twisting the cap to his water bottle on and off. "It hasn't happened here. And if it did happen, it would have to be when and where they are shipped. So far, we have not had any complaints about the packages being opened and then resealed. And we would have that."

"I see. How do you connect with Brit then other than what we have discovered? Were you in any classes together?" Bill was grasping at straws at that point to find a connection.

Rori shook his head. He and Richard had discussed that and he had approached Brit as well.

"None that we know of. We went off to different colleges. She was a year behind me in school." Rori sighed. "That's not what you wanted to hear, was it?"

"No, it wasn't." Bill studied Rori, seeing the stress that was etching lines in his face as well as the fatigue that he was showing. "Rori? You know at some point we'll need to put you two away together. I don't think that will be an option."

"I know that and so does Brit. She's fighting me on that, still not willing to acknowledge our marriage. And I don't know how to get her to understand." Rori looked up as he heard footsteps and Raleigh appeared. "Raleigh?"

"She understands that, Rori, better than you think. It's hard for her. She has had to pick up and raise her siblings while still a young woman. That has weighed heavily on her. Brit has not had the opportunity to be a young woman without responsibilities. She saw that coming in the near future. Now, that opportunity to date and find her life mate has been taken from her hands by someone who means you two harm. She's worried and scared."

Rori nodded at Raleigh's words. She was correct, he suspected, in how Brit was feeling.

"So, what do we do then, Raleigh? You had the experience of being forced to marry. At least, Richard was aware enough of what was going on to agree to it. I wasn't. That has to affect how Brit is feeling, thinking that we are both trapped by this with me not really understanding what was being asked of me or being able to fully agree."

"And there's that. All I can say is pray. Trust God in this. He is in control and is protecting you two. We don't always see this when we're in the midst of something, no matter how many times someone says that to us. Talk to her as you can. Pray with her. If you have to, court her as Richard would say."

"Court her?" Rori stared at her as she grinned at him, seeing Bill nodding in agreement. "That's what Andrew does with Phoebe and you with Cora, Bill?"

"It is, Rori. You are correct in that. For now, if you're done work, let's head off to find Brit. I need to speak with you both and I would like to do that together. Raleigh? Are you free to come with us? It might help for Brit to hear your story."

Raleigh shrugged. Richard had dropped her off with a promise to return if Rori couldn't drive her home.

"Sure. She needs to know that she is not alone in any of this. We need to get Phoebe in touch with her as well." Raleigh paused. "God is here, Rori. You know that." She reached to hug her brother, distressed that he was in danger, but glad in a way that Brit was in his life. If Brit would only stay in his life, that was. Not one of them expected that to happen.

Heading towards Brit's building, Bill was puzzled by all that had happened. This should not have, he knew, but someone somewhere in their town meant Rori and Brit harm. None of them had been able to come up with a reason other than Brit's work. And Edward Younge was not speaking. They had arrested him after Brit had been freed. They were finding out just what a nasty person Younge was and how deep into crime he was. Their feeling was that he was not the one causing this to the young couple. Bill wanted to solve it and solve it that day. That just wasn't happening. Emma had been in touch, sending what she could despite being involved in urgent investigations.

Turning as she heard Bill's voice speaking with her secretary, Brit sighed and stared down at her work. She couldn't stop at that point. Glancing at the clock, she knew that she had at least thirty minutes of work to finish off that project and finish it off she would. Brit nodded as Amy appeared beside her.

"Go on home, Amy. Bill will have to wait. I need to finish this assessment today." Brit was soon lost in her work, forgetting that she had people waiting for her. Thirty minutes later, she sat back. Her report was finished and emailed off to the customer before she was locking away her work and the jewels. Her face turned upright as she sighed, praying for strength for the next few days. It was Friday and she just wanted to hibernate in her home, not even seeing her siblings. That wouldn't happen, she knew.

Her steps slowed as she heard voices in the waiting room and sighed once more, praying for the strength that she needed and that her faith in God would be enough to get her through the next few days. Brit prayed that God would end whatever this was that weekend but knew that wouldn't likely happen.

Chapter 26

Hesitating as she reached the doorway to the reception area, Brit drew in a deep breath. Somehow, she knew that once she walked into that room, her life would once more change. She listened carefully to the voices and sighed once more. Rori just had to be there, didn't he? And she heard a female voice that she wasn't quite sure of.

Bill was on his feet as Brit appeared, assessing her and not liking what he was seeing. Brit was stressed, he could tell, and ready to run. The question in his mind was if she ran, would Rori run with her or after her. And that he could see Rori doing.

"Brit? Do you have a few moments?" Bill waited for her to speak.

"I would like to go home, Bill. It's been a long week and I need my home." Brit pointed to the door. "If you want to meet, we meet there." She refused to look at Rori, not seeing the understanding on his face or not Raleigh's face.

"We can do that. Ev wants to provide dinner for us. Avery's working tonight and will personally deliver it to wherever we are." Raleigh reached to hug Brit, finding Brit hugging her back and not seeming to want to let go. "We'll talk, Brit, you and I and then Richard's team as well as Phoebe, Cora, and Madigan. We've all had adventures that we didn't like and we need to share them. Rayleen would as well except that she and Riley are out of town. Can we meet sometime this weekend?"

Brit studied the lady just around her own age and then nodded. She needed to hear those stories, she knew, and God was providing a way for that to happen.

"Sure, I guess. Just set something up." Brit locked up her building and then headed for her car, not surprised that Rori was waiting for her. She looked at him and then at Bill, seeing Bill nodding at her. She turned as she heard the sound of tires on the pavement and sighed once more. He just had to bring in a patrol car, didn't he.

Bill searched the exterior of Brit's home, knowing full well that the men had been around. She had sent him their pictures that had been captured on her security system. Brit had not said anything and that concerned him. He was afraid that she was shutting down and when she did that, that's when she became less alert and more vulnerable to attack and being taken captive again.

Brit hesitated as she pulled on her comfy clothes as she termed them and reached for her phone. A smile crossed her face at the text messages from Becc and Bevan. They would be around over the weekend, and she just feared for them. She had no idea if whoever it was would go after them to get to her. She prayed for their safety, trying to think of where she could send them that would keep them safe.

Raleigh was waiting for Brit and once more simply hugged the lady. She knew that Rori was not walking away from Brit, no matter what Brit stated. Raleigh could see that her brother was in love with the lady in front of her. She just couldn't read Brit or her emotions.

Turning as he heard Brit's footsteps, Bill nodded to himself. She's trying to come up with a plan, he decided, but would she let them in on it? He didn't think that she would. Somehow, he had to get through to her that these men or women meant business. Her life and Rori's life was at stake. That was how they were all reading the situation. It was how it alway went, Bill knew.

"Bill? Why do we need to meet today?" Brit was not backing down from him. She sensed Rori moving to stand beside her, an arm around her. She jumped slightly as he did that, not expecting him to.

"We need to meet, Brit, with you and Rori as a couple." Bill's hand went up to stop her words. "For all intents and purposes, you two are a couple. Whether that continues or not, that's yours and Rori's decision. For now, we have to determine how to keep the two of you safe. And for now, that means you two are together, in the same house, when you are not working. Andrew has stated this must happen. If you don't, Brit, he is fully prepared to stick you away in a safe house out of town. You won't be working. You won't see Becc and Bevan. Your life will consist of four walls of a house that you can't even step outside of. And there's no guarantee that this would even work." Bill gave a compassionate smile as Brit fully and finally understood his words. "Work with us, Brit. Rori is willing to do that."

Brit's head turned as she studied the tall handsome man standing beside her. She knew his character just from the limited contact that she had had with him. She knew his family and their character. Her gaze then turned to Raleigh who was nodding.

"Raleigh?" Brit's voice was barely audible.

"It's what it is. All we are asking is that you stay with Rori until this is solved. It may not be for that long. It would also give you and Rori a chance to speak and decide what you want to do." Raleigh hesitated to continue, opened her mouth and then closed it. She had said what God wanted her to say. Anything else would be from her and that she couldn't do.

Rori's arm tightened around Brit. He knew the conflict that she was under. He felt the same. He wanted to court this lady who was his bride and win her love. He just didn't know if that would work.

"We need this, Brit. If we don't, then they'll go after our families to make it happen. I don't understand why. None of us do at this point." He sighed, the sigh sounding loud in the room. "I know that you don't want this. We would not restrict your access to your work. In fact, if needed, we have a room at the shop that we could set you up in a temporary way. Bill has offered off-duty officers to be with us when we are at work. That's an option that we need to pray about." Rori paused his words, seeing the look in Brit's eyes, a look that said she understood but asked where did they stand as a couple. He felt her body relax to some extent and knew then that she would agree.

"For how long, Bill?" Brit had to ask even though she was well aware of how long investigations could take.

"That we don't know, Brit. We are actively investigating. We have a lady who is investigating as well and sending us information. We just need that one piece to find the person responsible and then make the arrests. We have made arrests for those connected to Younge. He's not talking but the others are. That keeps this investigation alive."

Bill finally walked away, not happy that there had been no decision made in his presence. Raleigh locked the door after him and then stood, watching Rori and Brit face off. The only decision that they had to make was where they would live. And neither one seemed to be able to make that decision. A tap at the door had her turning back to it and into Richard's hug.

"How's it going?" Richard kept his voice low. He had spoken with his friends, Don and Abe, and knew that they would bring in their security teams if needed.

"Close to a decision, I think. I just don't know for sure." Raleigh looked up at Richard. "Can't we push them just a little?"

Richard smiled at her comment. That was why he was there. God had sent him to do just that.

Chapter 27

"Rori? Brit?" Richard's voice broke into the stare-off or face-off or whatever it was called that the couple were involved in. Richard watched as Brit jumped, a touch of fear crossing her face. He frowned. She had been threatened more than she had told anyone. "Brit? How often have you been receiving messages and threats?" He was refusing to let her away with this. It affected someone near and dear to his wife and that he would not allow to happen any longer.

Brit shrugged. The threats had been coming more frequently in the last few days. She had finally muted her phone, only checking it every couple of hours. She knew that Becc and Bevan would complain, but it was what it was.

"More frequently in the last couple of days. To my phone using my work number. I haven't had any packages if that's what you're asking. Those are next, aren't they?" Brit didn't look away from Rori, seeing his eyes close as she acknowledged the threats.

"Brit? Would you have told us?" Rori stared her down, seeing her gaze drop as she thought through what he had asked.

Brit shrugged, not willing to admit that she likely would not have told them. She had deleted the messages, not willing to acknowledge how scared that she really was.

"I don't know, Rori. They threatened me and my siblings. Not you. So you tell me why? Why were you kidnapped and then put in that hole? It's where we usually walk. That was done on purpose, you know." Her hands were up to shove him away from her before she walked away from the kitchen and the three standing and staring after her.

Raleigh shrugged before she followed Brit, simply to sit beside her on the loveseat in her home office. Brit didn't speak, not sure what she could even say that would make sense.

"How did you do it, Raleigh?" Brit's voice was broken, her emotions finally breaking through the strict hold and guard that she had on them.

"It was hard, Brit. Richard and I were married. We chose to honour that commitment to one another even though we were strangers. We are deeply in love." Her hand rested on her abdomen, feeling their little one moving slightly. "Rori out there? He will not walk away from you, despite you walking away from him. He'll just hang around in the shadows, keeping watch as he can for you. And that places him in danger even more. You know that. What we need to do is to determine why. What wold have caused this?"

Brit shrugged, her thoughts going back to her work and the requests that she had received. She didn't take all the requests, refusing a number. She frowned.

"There was a request about three months ago. It didn't make any sense, what they were asking. I just ignored it." Brit was on her feet, moving rapidly towards her filing cabinet. "I print off each request and then decide from there what I want to do." She held out the folder, her eyes on Richard as he reached for it. "I didn't get a good feeling for what they were asking and just set it aside. I guess that I shouldn't have but I get these kinds of requests all the time."

Richard nodded. It was the same for his security team, particularly now that they were only doing training. He could understand to some extent why she had set it aside. He opened the folder and read through the few pieces of paper inside it before he looked up.

"You have no idea who this is?" As Brit shook her head in the negative, Richard nodded. "I know of him. He is into crime, which you not likely knew. Let me take this to my team and we'll work on it. I'll also send it on to Emma, who will look into him. Bill needs a copy as well. May I pass it on to him?" Richard waited patiently for Brit to respond, not willing to override her wishes at that point.

Brit's eyes were on Rori who had stopped beside Richard, his eyes on the name

"He's been around our place, Richard. About six months ago. He was wanting to invest in the company. Dad sent him on his way." Rori's eyes slid closed. "That's why. Revenge?"

"That's a distinct possibility." Richard shared a look with Raleigh. "We'll work it like we did for everyone else. For now, though, where are you two going to live? I would suggest here, Rori. Brit has a really good security system, one of the best that I have seen. You have one but we would need to really upgrade it and we should."

Rori kept his eyes on Brit, not sure which way she was leaning in the decision. He saw the moment that she gave in and nodded. He was across the room, wrapping her into a hug, knowing that she was not happy with that decision but also knew she was well aware that they had to make it.

"Brit? Here?" Rori felt her nod against him. "It's not going to be for that long, I pray." His head went down as he prayed for his lady, bringing in all the verses that he could that talked of protection, hope, God's love, and then prayed just for her.

Brit had stiffened as he prayed for her and then relaxed against the man who was holding her. She sensed that their relationship was changing at that point. She could feel the care, concern, and yes, love that Rori was trying so hard to let her know.

Stepping back from Rori, Brit studied the man who would now be in her home all the time. She wasn't ready for that but she had to acknowledge that she was afraid, deeply afraid. The threats getting worse and worse with each one.

"When?" Brit's voice was barely audible.

"Today, Brit." Richard gave her a small smile, showing her that he understood. "We'll make it work, Brit. For now, Rori's here. Someone will go through your building and up the security there even though you state that it is strong. You may need to work off site from there. Can you do that?"

Brit shook her head. It wasn't that easy to move what she needed.

"I can't. I have to work there. It's really difficult to move what I need to do." Brit sighed. "And I have a backlog of work that I need to be at."

"No working seven days a week for now, Brit. We need to restrict how long you are there. Not when it is dark. You go in during daylight and leave during daylight." Richard's hand went up at her protect. "We need to do that, Brit. It's too dangerous for you otherwise."

Chapter 28

Rori turned late that afternoon, hearing his parents speaking with Becc and Bevan. They had appeared not that long ago, greeted him, and then looked for Brit, not finding her. She was hiding, Rori knew, ashamed at their marriage. They had begun to talk, those two, and that had been one thing that she had stated. They had had no choice, he knew, but it still weighed heavy on the two of them.

Brit stood for a moment just inside the back door, watching her groom. She sighed. This was not how she had ever expected to marry. In fact, she had been adamant that she never would. Brit had planned to close her business once Becc and Bevan were settled and simply leave town, not telling anyone where she was going. She needed a break and that didn't seem to be happening. Brit had questioned God long and hard as to why but He had been silent for the moment. She knew that she had to wait for Him and that was hard as a human to wait on Someone she couldn't see.

Rori turned as he heard Brit's soft movements. He frowned for a moment, not sure how to approach her.

"Brit?" Rori stopped in front of her, bending over to look into her beautiful face.

"Rori? Did we really agree to this?"

"We did. We don't have any option, Brit. You know that." Rori reached to hug her, finding her returning the hug, something that she had not done in the past. "We'll get there."

"I know, but who will be hurt in the process?" Brit leaned against Rori, not hearing the soft footsteps as Rori's mother hesitated as she walked into the room.

"We'll take all the precautions that we can, love. You know that. Richard's team will be around when they can. Bill has offers from fellow officers to work with us on their off time. There are also two other security teams that will move in if we need them."

"And you think that we will?" Brit looked up at him, frowning at that thought.

"We may, love. We may. We'll decide on that together unless something is really drastically wrong and we are in more danger that we can handle. We'll pray this through."

"I know that we will. It just seems that God is not hearing my prayers." Brit shoved away from him, turning to walk back outside.

Rori stared after her, wanting to go with her but knowing that he had to let her have this time. Rebekah stopped her hug her son before she followed Brit, simply sitting beside her on the wicker love seat, not saying anything but praying hard for her daughter-in-law.

"Rebekah?" Brit spoke at last, her gaze following the flight of some geese as they flew overhead.

"Brit? You are lost in what you are facing. This is when you need your mom and dad and don't have them. Let Ross and I step in, not to take their place, but to be there for you and Rori. What can we do for you?" Rebekah watched with compassion as Brit's composure broke and she sobbed. Rebekah's arms were around the younger lady, a mother prayer whispering out loud for her.

"I need my Mom." Brit's voice was barely a whisper. "I need my Dad. He would stop this." Brit moved away from Rebekah, a hand up to swipe at her face and at the tears that still flowed. "Why is this happening?"

"I don't know why, Brit, but I do know that God is using this for His glory. He is using you and Rori to bring someone to justice. We don't always like or appreciate how He works. God is in control, never doubt that. He loves you more than that son of mine does and more than your siblings do."

Brit stared at her as she continued to speak, her mind not moving past the comment that Rori loved her. That wasn't possible, she decided. It was too soon. She was unlovable, or so she thought. Someone had pushed that hard at her over the years and she wanted to know why.

"I think I know who it is. He's related to Younge but is around Richard's age. He has always chased me and tried to beat me down, since we were kids. I don't understand why." Brit looked up as Rori sat on the table in front of her, reaching for her hands. "Rori?"

Rori simply stated a name, nodding as she paled and then agreed with him. Raleigh had had issues with the same man over the years and others had as well, he knew. They had just never been able to stop him.

"I'll give his name to Bill, although I am sure that he has already found this name." Rori reached to hug his lady, finding her responding this time without hesitation. He nodded as his mother rose and walked away, knowing that he did indeed need to speak with his lady. He had listened as his mother had counselled Brit, not wanting to intrude until he had to.

Brit looked up at him, a frown on her face. Now that the name was out there, they had to find a way to stop him. And it had to be her, didn't it, Lord? She was afraid, more afraid than she had ever been.

"Rori?" Brit's voice was hesitant as she continued to watch him.

"I do love you, Brit, more than anyone else. I thought it was too soon to tell you." Rori refused to look at Brit, not wanting to see her refusal of his declaration. His hands pushed at the table, preparatory to his rising but he stopped as her hand touched his arm.

"Do you mean that, Rori?" Brit waited for him to give an abrupt nod. "I don't know how I feel about you but thank you. We need to get through this and then talk."

"We'll talk, Brit, and before this is over." Rori rose, dropped a kiss to her forehead, and then walked away, knowing that Brit needed time to ponder what she had been told. He just didn't know how much time that they would have.

Ross approached his son later that day as Rori stood in his own home, staring around. His duffle bags were packed with what he needed. Only he wasn't sure that he could do this, move in with Brit.

"Son?" Ross reached to hug his tall son, trying to think of how Rori had grown so quickly and so tall. It seemed like just yesterday that Rori was a newborn baby placed into his arms for the first time. "What can we do for you?" Ross had not told Rori about the package that he had found on the back porch, instead just calling Bill to come and retrieve it. He knew that Bill would be around once it had been examined.

"Dad? How do we do this? I love her but I don't know it she'll ever love me back." Rori blinked against sudden tears, not sure why he was weeping, but knowing that his emotions were in a turmoil. He was also deeply afraid for his lady.

"With prayer and our support. You and Brit are not alone in this." Ross' arm rested around his son's shoulders as he prayed for him. "Come on, son. Let's get you to the love of your life." He gave a small sad smile as Rori finally nodded and reached for some of his bags.

Chapter 29

Brit ran for her home two days later. She had left work early, stopping to grab some groceries, but feeling very uncomfortable as she moved through the store. Someone was stalking her, she knew. Brit just didn't know who. Everyone she saw was from her town.

Her hand was shaking almost too much to find the lock with her key. Once inside, and the security system turned off, Brit rested against the door, her hand still holding the bags from the grocery store. She finally moved towards the kitchen, an eye on the clock. If Rori kept to his schedule, he would be home soon and she had to make their meal. She just didn't feel like it.

The vibrating of her phone startled her. It had been doing that off and on all day and the messages were getting more and more brutal. Those she had forwarded to Bill but had not heard back from him as yet. She smiled as she read the message from Rori, a simple one to say that he loved her and that he was stopping at Ev's diner to pick up a meal. Was she safe? Her fingers flew across the keyboard as she responded before she was setting away the groceries and then heading to change. Brit's hand rested on a favourite sweatshirt before she shrugged. She didn't dress fancy even for work and tonight? Tonight she needed her comfort clothes.

Rori turned as he heard Brit's footsteps, reaching to draw her into a hug, not finding her resisting him as she usually did. Something had happened, he decided, that day which caused the change. He would ask her but first, they needed to eat and then spend time in prayer.

Drawing Brit down beside him on the living room couch, Rori did not let her move away from him. His arm tightened on her as she tried even as his head bowed and he began to pray for them both.

Brit raised her head at last, grateful that Rori was a Christian who strongly believed in prayer. That had been how she was raised and how she had gotten through the years since her parents had died. She bit at her lip, knowing that she had to speak with him about that day.

"Brit? What happened today?" Rori didn't look directly at her, instead tightening his arm around the lady he loved.

"Someone was following me in the grocery store and then when I came home. I couldn't see anyone who seemed out of place." Brit was angry at that, angry that she was in such a situation as they were.

"That's what they do. They monitor our activities and who we are with. Was anyone with you?" Rori sighed as Brit shook her head. "There was supposed to be. An officer was assigned to be outside of your building."

"There wasn't anyone there, Rori. And that's what I thought Bill said. Who got to them?" Brit struggled to move away from Rori until she could find her phone. Seated beside him once more, she sent off a text to Bill and then to Lily, not wanting to know that someone had gotten to the officer.

Bill turned as Lily called his name. They were both leaving for the day but Bill had been hesitating for some reason.

"Lily?" Bill watched the anger that flickered across her face.

"John, the officer assigned to Brit today, is missing. She said that there was no one outside when she left and that she was followed as she shopped and then went home." Lily was afraid that John had sold them out as the saying went.

"John? Missing? That's not John. He was adamant that he had to be there today." Bill ran for his vehicle, seeing Lily running for her.

Parked outside of Brit's building, Bill and Lily began their search even as dusk was falling. They stood at last beside Bill's car, not seeing the patrol car or John.

"Where is he?" Lily spun in a circle before she was running for the building next door, a ramshackle building that had been abandoned. She searched before her voice was calling for Bill, who had followed her. "Here's John. He's alive but hurt."

Brit stepped back from her front door as Bill approached, a look on his face that she didn't like. She could hear Rori moving around in the kitchen, preparing coffee for them.

"Bill?" Brit waited as he stood for a moment, staring at her before his head shook. "The officer?"

"We found him, Brit. He was taken out so that someone could get to you. He was in the building next to you. For now, he's unconscious and hasn't been able to say what happened to him. You saw nothing?" Bill searched her face, seeing the devastation that she was feeling at the thought that John had been hurt.

"No, I didn't." Brit turned and walked for the kitchen, her hand reaching for the mug of coffee Rori held out to her before she sat, burying her face in her hands.

Rori watched her, a hand on her shoulder before he was facing Bill.

"Bill?"

Bill sighed, his portfolio dropping to the wooden tabletop before he reached for the mug waiting for him. He sat, not saying anything. He watched Rori and then Brit before he shook his head. The attraction towards one another was there but Brit was hiding hers. Rori was not and that could be a problem, Bill knew.

"Okay, you two. Here's where it comes down to it." Bill waited for the couple to respond. "Ignoring me won't work, Brit. Been there. Done that. So for now? You two are together." His hand went up as she protested. "It's not an option any more, Brit. You have seen the way that you are watched. You left at an unusual time for you to do so today. That saved you. What is it that they want from you?"

Brit shrugged. She had been puzzling that over and over and could not come to a definite reason.

"They wanted me to manufacture gems. I don't do that." Brit frowned at Rori as his mouth opened and closed. "Rori?"

"That's not it, Brit. We all know that you don't do that. You investigate gems and value them. What if they wanted you to investigate and value real gems and then switch them after you had done that? Would that be why?"

Bill was nodding. That had been a discussion that the detectives had had at their early morning meeting. The consensus was that was the case and that Brit was in deep danger.

"Rori? Where all do you ship your glass works?" Bill's attention turned to Rori, seeing the instance that he understood.

"They would use our parcels for the real gems and smuggle them out? I don't see how that would work unless there was someone at the post office involved and even then there would be no guarantee that they would be able to do that. We don't package our products until the day that they ship and then one of us hand delivers them to the post office. It's what we've always done." Rori's head went back as he groaned. "We use the new employees to do that and we have had some new employees come on staff." He reached for a pad of paper and a pen, hastily scrawling down the names before he shoved the paper at Bill. "These are the newest ones but look into everyone."

"We will do that." Bill stood at last, not content that he had reached through to either one, particularly Brit.

Chapter 30

Brit paced through her home early the next morning. She was scared, she had to admit, more scared than she had been. Vicious messages had been coming to her work phone and also her work email. Brit had forwarded them on to Bill, not caring that it was still early in the morning. She had heard no sound from Rori, the door to his bedroom still closed.

Walking outside of her home, Brit paused as she saw an officer rising from a chair on the back deck. She had not been aware that Bill had arranged that.

"You're here early." Brit stopped beside the officer. "I have coffee on if you want one."

"I was here all night, Brit." Joe shook his head. "You didn't know?"

"No, Bill never said. And he should have." Brit's focus was on the yard before she was marching down the grass to the garden at the back of the yard. She stared down at the box sitting there before she felt Joe's hand moving her away. "When did that get here?"

"Sometime overnight or late yesterday afternoon. They are watching you that close, Brit, and it doesn't matter to them that an officer was here. Back into the house." Joe almost shoved Brit inside, finding Rori waiting inside the door to wrap Brit into a hug. "Rori? Both of you stay inside." He was gone, the door closed behind him, before Rori would even ask a question.

"Brit? What was that about?" Rori didn't release it and Brit didn't move away from him. Instead, Rori found her relaxing against him.

"A box. Someone put a box at the end of the yard even though Joe was here." She frowned up at Rori, seeing something in his eyes that she was special and that he loved her. Brit shoved at him, moving away to grab her mug of coffee.

"They did? And he's called it in? Then, we wait." Rori gave a small smile as she spun and frowned at him. "We have to, Brit. We have no idea what it is or who placed it. They'll assess it and then reach out to us." He held out his hand. "Come on, sweetheart. Let's find a corner for our prayer corner."

Brit continued to frown at him. There was no way that they had a prayer corner together. That wasn't possible. As soon as they were out of danger, she was walking away from him. Only, God was not letting her do that, not just yet. She sighed to herself. Yes, God was in control and for some reason, He had brought Rori into her life. Brit just didn't like it. She preferred her solo life, despite the tears that she had shed at night because of that. Deep in her heart, she wanted that one man, a knight, to walk into her life and rescue her from that said loneliness.

Walking into the living room, Brit stared around before she found the chair that was her favourite. Sitting, she stared at Rori as he chose a chair near her, his hand reaching for hers and grasping it tightly before his head bowed and he began to pray. Brit's own head bowed as she listened to his prayer, feeling as if she had been brought right into God's presence in heaven.

She frowned at how he ended his prayer, with an "I love You".

"Rori?" Brit waited somewhat impatiently until he lifted his head, a smile on his face just for her. "How you ended your prayer? That's unusual."

"It is. I picked up that habit from Richard. He always does that. When questioned, Richard always says that God needs to hear that we love Him and that is one way that we can do that."

Brit studied Rori, seeing the strength of his character and also the strength and depth of his Christian walk. She needed that at this time, she knew.

"How long do you think this will take, whatever it is that we are mixed up in?" Brit was desperate to move on and let Rori move on.

"I don't know. I do know that Richard's team and their spouses are meeting today to work on this mystery. It's what they do. Riley and Rayleen will be there. I heard that Lily and Loch will be as well, just as friends." Rori studied her. "We'll get you there, sweetheart." He looked around as he heard the back door open and close and then footsteps heading their way. "Joe?"

"It wasn't a bomb, Brit, Rori. Instead, it seems as if someone is trying to help you." Joe set the box down, a puzzled look on his face. "Bill had the team take photos for him and then sent this in to you. He's been called to another crime scene but said he'd touch base with you two later."

Brit shook her head, her hands waving in the air as she walked away. She didn't need this right now, she decided. Rori was hovering and trying to protect her. She didn't need that, she didn't think, not realizing the danger that was encroaching on the two of them and that would strike within days.

Rori stared after Brit for a moment before he turned to the box, his hands reaching for the photos and then laying them out. He frowned at them. Bill was right. There was no threat, just photos of Rori and Brit together. Unless? Rori had his phone out, capturing the photos and then forwarding them on to Richard. He turned at last to stand in the kitchen doorway, looking towards the bedrooms, not wanting to disturb Brit but knowing that he had to at some point. She really needed to see these photos. What Rori didn't know was at that moment Brit was involved in a struggle with God over her relationship with Rori.

Brit sat on the side of her bed, her head bowed, tears on her face. She was struggling to accept the fact that she was indeed married when she didn't want to be. God had allowed it, she knew, and that was part of her struggled, understanding and accepting that God was in control of this portion of her life. She knew that God only wanted the best for her and that He had plans and purposes for this. Brit just didn't want it. She finally was silent, knowing that she had to wait for God to speak to her, surrendering her will to His.

At last, Brit arose and walked into the ensuite, staring at herself in the mirror. She could see the struggles that she had just undergone showing on her face. A hand reached for her washcloth to rinse it out under as hot of water as she could stand before she was scrubbing at her face.

God had answered her, asking her if she truly trusted Him. His voice echoed in her ears that her surrender to His will was all that He was asking. She felt His love surrounding her at that point as she accepted His plan. Brit knew that she had to face Rori, just not wanting to.

Her hand rested against the closed bedroom door for a moment as her head once more bowed. She knew that she would still struggle with the decision that she had reached, that it impacted more than just herself.

Chapter 31

Watching as Brit walked towards him, Rori felt a sense of extreme danger approaching the house. He reached for her hand, rushing her through the kitchen, the box picked up and carried with them. Rori had Brit out of the house and into his truck, driving away as rapidly as he could, not seeing the shocked look on her face.

"Rori?" Brit could hear the hesitation in her voice as she spoke his name before she was staring behind her. "What was that all about?"

Rori shrugged. He didn't know how to explain his feelings to her.

"I'm not sure, Brit. I felt God's hand on us, shoving us from the house." He shot a look at her, seeing the fear on her face and hating it. "I've learned to listen to those nudges. We would have likely disappeared again." He held out his phone to her. "Here. Call it in to Bill or Jason, please. They need to be at our home." His attention went back to the road and his drive to Richard's home.

Brit shot him a quick glance before she dialed the police line, not asking for either of the men who Rori had named, just stating that they felt something or someone at her home. And no, they were not there. Rori had made them leave and if they needed to reach them, they would be at Richard's. She hung up before much more could be asked of her.

Setting his phone in the cup portion of the centre console, Brit studied Rori, seeing once more the steady and sincere character of her groom. She sighed, knowing that her heart was opening up to him and that she still was not sure about. Only God would give her peace about that.

"Rori? Who is after us? And which one is it?" Brit wasn't clear on that in her mind at all.

"I don't know, Brit. I'm sorry. I really wish that I did now. And I do wish that I could remember what happened before you found me." Rori parked at Richard's office building, knowing that would be where they were meeting. He shifted on his seat, his hands reaching for hers. He studied those hands, his thumbs rubbing along the back of them. He frowned for a moment, not finding that Brit was moving away from him. "I really do wish things had been different. You deserved the chance and the right to choose who you would marry and go through all the fun stuff leading up to a wedding that you planned." He felt a gentle tug from her hands and looked up at her, sensing that she had made a decision

"It is what it is, Rori. We can't change that." Brit bit at her lip, a sign that she was uncertain. "We'll talk, I promise, and decide together what we want to do. For now, I see Richard watching us and waiting for us to come in."

Rori gave a brief grin, before he was around the truck, and helping her down. He reached for the box of photos and then for her hand, not finding her resisting that. Rori studied her, seeing a peace that she had now that had not been present earlier. He could only beg God that she stayed with him, his love for her overflowing in his heart and into his eyes.

Richard reached for the box as Rori handed it to him, not sure what it was.

"Those are photos of us. That box appeared in the back yard this morning. Bill has seen them." Rori held the door for Brit, watching as she disappeared, Silver and Naomi, the two ladies on Richard's security team, walking towards her. "I fear for her, Richard. I just don't know how to do this."

"Yes, you will fear for her. And no, you don't know how to do this. Even those of us who are in law enforcement of some kind had difficulty knowing what to do. It's different when it's someone you love who is in danger and you don't know who or why." Richard watched with compassion as Rori hesitated to enter the building. "What else happened?"

"I felt such a sense of evil and danger as we were leaving. I just rushed Brit from her home and to here. She did call it in. I suspect that someone will track us down at some point." Rori entered the building, finding his sister waiting for him. He hugged her, not wanting to let go but knowing that he had to. "Raleigh?"

"It's okay, Rori. Your lady is with our ladies. Now, what about you?" Raleigh looked up at her brother, studying him. "You're still in danger. I want this over for you."

Rori gave a quick grin before he looked up to see Brit standing behind Raleigh and waiting for him. He reached for her hand, hesitation in his movements.

"Brit?" His voice held a question that she just shook her head at. Now was not the time to talk. That would come.

"It's okay, Rori. We just were looking for you three. I gather we're meeting for prayer before we start anything. And there are a lot of people here that I don't know."

Rori peeked into the largest conference room and gave a low laugh. There were indeed a number of people there, including Richard's long-time friend, Don, and his team and their spouses, as well as another friend from another town, Abe and his team and their spouses. He was glad to see Abe's wife, Emma, there. She had a business where she found people and information that no one else could. Rori suspected that she had a pile of information for them.

Brit wandered along the edge of the conference room, reading the white boards, surprised at how much information was already on them. She frowned at some of the notes, not sure where the information had come from.

Silver and Naomi paced with her, knowing that she would have questions and willing to help her understand as best as they could. They could sense the fear that she was tamping down, having gone through adventures of their own as they were termed.

"Brit? What do we need to do for you to help you understand this?" Naomi's hand on Brit's arm finally stopped the other lady in her tracks.

"What do you need to do? Solve this." Brit rubbed at her face. "This should never have happened.

I don't understand why. And I don't understand how you've managed to find so much information all ready." Brit turned as she felt an arm around her and faced a lady who she didn't know.

"I'm Emma, Brit. And I guess it's my fault for some of this information. I find people and info that others can't." Emma grinned at her for a moment. "And yes, Abe and I did have an adventure."

Brit studied the older lady who really wasn't that much older that she was, she didn't think.

"Then, you can explain it to me in a way that I can understand. Ask me about gems and I can tell you. This?" Brit waved a hand at the boards. "I'm lost. And here is Rori to ask the same questions." She felt Rori's arms around her, tugging her back against him. This time? She leant back on him, not surprising him when she did so.

Chapter 32

Brit studied the paperwork dropped on the table in front of her, a finger flicking at the pile. She had no idea how this much information had been found, but it had been and now she was faced with the daunting task of reading through it. She sighed. This was not how her day was to have been. Brit had had plans to leave town for a few days, needing a break, but that hadn't happened. She was too worried about Bevan and Becc. Besides, Rori would have had to come with her and that would not have been the escape that she needed.

Rori set a mug of coffee beside her pile of paper and then pulled out a chair to sit beside her. He could tell that she was overwhelmed, just by her attitude and how she was sitting.

"Brit? Let's pray first before we start going through that." Rori didn't want for her to respond. Instead, he simply bowed his head and prayed, his hand tightening on Brit's. He frowned as he finished. This time? She had not tried to remove her hand from his and that surprised him. He looked sideways at her, seeing that she still sat with her head bowed and her eyes closed. "Brit?" His voice was low, only loud enough for Brit to hear him.

"It's okay, Rori." Brit looked up, peace on her face. "God and I have come to an understanding. I mean, I understand what He wants even though it's not what I want. Now, what is all this?" She lifted a corner of the pile and let it drop again.

Rori grinned at her even as he tried to understand what she was saying.

"Emma has been busy as has friends of hers. Our friends have been as well. This is what they would have found and yes, Bill and his detectives would have most of what it there. What they won't have is what is not proven or there are questions that we need to clarify our answers for. This is how we work." Rori tightened his hand on hers. "And we do need to talk. I am glad for the peace that I see."

"Thank you." Brit bit at her lip. "I'm not sure if I'm completely convince that this is right, you and I, but God doesn't seem to be saying no to anything that we're doing."

"No, He's not. And He would. Just remember that we have been prayed for in the garden. God has walked this path before us, knowing from before time began what we would face. And He is right here with us now."

"I know that but it is sometimes hard to comprehend and understand in my humanness." Brit reached for the pile of papers, a pen in her hand as she began to read and make notes.

An hour later, Brit looked up, seeing Rori still immersed in his reading. She was on her feet, a notepad in her hand as she paced, studying the notes that she had made. Silver approached her, reaching for the pad and pen and setting them one side.

"Let's walk outside, Brit. You need that. And yes, there are some of the guys out there." Silver linked an arm with Brit, leading from the building and to walk around it. "I love this place. Richard has done a lot over the years. You would never know that they had to rebuild his house when it was bombed."

"It was bombed?" Brit stared at the house. "I didn't know that. Or maybe I did. There has just been some much going on lately."

"There has been, and you have been looking after your family. Now, it's time for you." Silver looked behind her. "Rori is out here, watching you. He's in love with you, Brit."

"I know and I don't want to hurt him. I just don't know how to feel. Not any more." Brit was sober as she spoke. "I never expected to marry, not ever, and especially not as we were forced to. Rori can't remember anything about it. And that's not right." Brit felt arms around her and knew that Rori had approached her. She still was unsettled in her mind as to how she felt about him. She knew how she would have felt if he had approached her on his own with a view to dating. That had been taken away from both of them.

"What all do you remember?" Rori's voice sounded from behind her.

"What do I remember? About what? Or rather who?"

"The Younges. I have not had a lot of contact with them." Rori turned her back towards the office building, an arm around her to keep her from running. A puzzled look crossed his face as she didn't make that attempt this time.

"The Younges? There have always been rumours that they are involved in crime. He had two brothers. Each of them have five children. The brothers have three boys and two girls. Edward has three girls and two boys. They would be around our age or younger." Brit sat back down in her chair, finding a fresh mug of coffee and a bagel waiting for her. She sighed. Someone was taking care of her and that someone was Rori. He was just wiggling his way into her heart, now wasn't he? And Brit knew that God was working in her own heart to open it for Rori.

Abe shared a look with Emma before he sat beside her, Emma between them.

"Emma has been finding out a lot about them, Brit. But they are not the head of this crime organization. And that is what it is." Abe shared a look with both Don and Richard. They all knew the man and what he was involved it. That concerned them enough that they had gone to Bill and Andrew to make preliminary plans if they were needed.

"I know that it is." Brit sighed. "And I don't know why. It's like I learned that before I really knew what it was and can't forget it. Only there hasn't been enough evidence or people willing to come forward to charge them. It just had to be Rori and I." The men with her smiled tightly at her plaintive words. "And how do we go about proving this?"

"My team is working through that, Brit, and finding evidence which we are passing on to the detectives in whatever jurisdiction it needs to go to. For now, we need to determine just why you were picked and why Rori was picked." Emma frowned for a moment, lost in thought.

"I don't know why, Emma. I knew of Rori from church but I don't know that we had ever crossed paths except for the occasional meeting. And even then, I don't remember speaking with Rori ever."

"We never have, Brit. We have sat close to one another at times but any committee we've been on? We were paired up with someone else." Rori was becoming very frustrated at not knowing why. He turned as Raleigh spoke from beside him, her hand resting on her brother's shoulders. "What was that, Raleigh?"

They all stared at Raleigh as she spoke, giving names and reasons. The group then shared a look before they settled back into the investigation. Perhaps Raleigh's perspective would aid in finding what they needed. Rori looked up to see Emma nodding at his sister's words and sighed. This had just grown the investigation at a time when they were trying to shrink it.

Chapter 33

Running for the door to her building, Brit struggled with her keys, trying to find the one that would unlock the door and let her escape whoever it was that was chasing her. She felt herself falling forward as she was tackled to the ground and then fists and feet pounding at her body. Despite curling up as small as she could, Brit could not escape the assault. The man walked away, content that he had done what he had been hired to do, and that was to hurt Brit for refusing to go along with his employer. The man stopped as he faced the three men standing in front of him.

Richard, Timothy, and Stephen had been too late to prevent the assault on Brit, arriving just as the man was leaving. Stephen, the paramedic on the team, brushed by the man and was on his knees beside Brit, assessing her. He looked up as Richard stood beside him.

"Stephen?"

"It's brutal, Richard. Thank God we were here so quickly. I just wish we had been here sooner." Stephen's attention went back to Brit, leaving Richard to stare down at her and then around as he heard the emergency personnel moving their way.

Bill stood an hour later, listening as the emergency room physician spoke with Rori. Rori had been horrified when Bill had tracked him down just as he had arrived at the studio. He had shaken his head that Brit had been hurt before he was almost running for Bill's car, leaving his father standing with a hand in the air as he reached to stop Rori.

"Soft tissue injuries are what we are seeing, Rori." The physician was well acquainted with Rori from church. Dr. Tim Walker was a friend to many of his fellow church members. "Brit likely has a concussion and won't be working for a few days. No internal injuries or bleeding that we can see."

"When can I take her home, Tim?" Rori's hand rested agains Brit's cheek.

"Soon. She has been rousing since she came in. We'll need to assess her before we let her go." Tim walked away, not looking back and not seeing the slumping of Rori's shoulders as he stood beside his wife.

"This wasn't to have happened, Bill. I hear that you have the man in custody." Rori didn't look up as Bill stopped at the end of the stretcher.

"We do. And he's not talking. About what we expected." Bill studied his friend. "I'll be back around or Lily or Jason will. We need her statement before she leaves."

"That you do. Go on about what you need to. I'll call when she wakes up." Rori didn't look up as Bill walked away.

Bill looked backwards towards his friend before he spoke to Lily.

"Lily? You're staying?"

Lily nodded, her own eyes watching the couple. She hesitated before she spoke to Bill, knowing that her words would not bring comfort to anyone.

"I plan on it. Brit is becoming a friend but she is a victim and we need to try and keep her safe. It just isn't working out that well." Lily walked away, into the examination room and then up to the stretcher, causing Rori to jump as she did so.

Rori jumped as he heard footsteps, his head raising as he stared at Lily before he nodded. He turned as he heard other footsteps and his father's arm was around his shoulders as Ross prayed for his son. Richard stood on his other side, a hand resting on his shoulder as well.

"My team's here, Rori. Silver's in the room with Brit. The rest of us are around." Richard walked away, his heart raising in prayer for the lady who was not rousing at all, or not as they had hoped that she would.

"Richard?" Stephen spoke from where he had stopped in front of his boss.

"Stephen? Thanks. Everyone's here?"

"We are. Timothy and Naomi are in the waiting room. I'm heading outside shortly. Silver's already in with Brit." Stephen looked around, feeling watched but not seeing anyone. "How is she?"

"They're not sure yet, I don't think. We'll need to go over their home security once more. And then try and convince Brit that she really does need our help." Richard gave a wry smile as Stephen laughed at that.

"Good luck on that is all I can say, Richard. She's independent. What about Becc and Bevan?" Stephen hadn't seen her siblings.

"They've been away at a conference. I spoke with Bevan. They were heading home this afternoon but instead are now planning on leaving. Bill was aware of that and has sent someone to escort them. Whoever this is? They will go after those two to get to Brit. And I worry about Raleigh right now, that someone will go after her to get to Rori."

"And they might. Don's team is around your place. He had the same thought. He's willing to stay for the next week if you need him." Stephen walked away, leaving Richard deep in thought before that man turned to stare back into the room.

Richard shook his head, walking away to find Don waiting for him. The two team leaders headed for the cafeteria, needing to meet and make some plans, and that at present seemed the best place to be.

Don hesitated before his head bowed and he prayed for the friend sitting across the table from him. They had been friends since toddlers and even though they now lived in different towns, they kept in close contact. Both had walked into the other's lives when they had undergone their adventures with their teams and their spouses.

"Don? What are your thoughts? You know this town." Richard sipped at his mug of coffee, his eyes on the plate of food sitting in front of him. "Why did I order this? I am really not that hungry."

Don grinned at him, a soft laugh coming from him. He knew only too well how Richard was somewhat feeling.

"We need to eat, Richard. We both have been through this. I went through this with my sister, Daci." Don studied the few people in the cafeteria, focusing on a couple sitting near them who seemed too interested in what they were discussing. "We have a couple to your right who seems to be too interested in what we're discussing."

"I see that. For now, let's concentrate on what God is doing and how we can help Rori and Brit that way. When we're alone with our team, we'll discuss security." Richard sighed. He was exhausted and not just from this. He needed a vacation and that wasn't coming. Richard would not walk away from family when they were in danger.

Chapter 34

Moving carefully, Brit reached for clean clothes. This was not how her day was to have been, and she wanted the man responsible for her injuries. Rori had carried her into the house and to her bedroom, setting her carefully on her feet. He didn't have to speak. His emotions was open on his face and that troubled Brit. She knew that he cared deeply for her, just by his actions.

Hearing Becc's voice, Brit moved towards her bedroom door, pulling down the sweatshirt that she had donned. Opening the door, Brit watched as Becc stared at her before carefully reaching to hug her sister.

"Are you okay?" Becc's voice was barely audible.

"No, Becc, I'm not. This has gone far enough. I am so afraid for you and Bevan." Brit stared past her sister, seeing Rori waiting for her. She simply moved towards him, finding him moving her way to wrap her into his arms as tightly as he could. Brit finally had to acknowledge to herself that she did indeed love Rori. She just wished it had been her choice to begin with but then God had made the choice or allowed it to happen. They were a couple because of God and that she could live with. His ways were past understanding, at least on earth.

"Brit?" Rori sensed something different about her and leaned back to stare down at her. He frowned at the look on her face before he glanced around to see that they were on their own. He just couldn't help himself. Rori just had to kiss her, finding her responding.

"We'll talk, Rori, but for now, I could use a coffee and some toast." Brit made no effort to move away from him, her head resting against him. "Who's all here?"

"My family. Your family. Richard and some of his team are inside. The other two are outside. Don is here with his team as well, all outside." Rori simply held his lady. "You scared me, Brit. I thought that I had lost you."

"Not yet you haven't. They tried hard. I spoke with Bill a bit ago. He's frustrated that he can't find out any more information. Emma is trying as well but she's not finding what she needs on Younge other than what we've found."

Rori nodded, knowing that was the case.

"Then, it has to be someone other than Younge. And how do we figure that out?" He looked down as Brit moved slightly, seeing how pale her face had become, the bruising starting to show more and more. "Brit?"

"I have an idea who it is and I don't like it one bit." Brit looked up at the fellow who held her and held her love. "Let's eat and then pray. Then, I'll speak."

Rori refused to let her go, instead just holding her until Brit sighed and said the name. He stared at her and then down the hallway before he nodded. He was in agreement with her on that name. They just had to prove it and prove it they would.

Ross looked up as they finished their time of prayer, feeling God's presence near them. He frowned at his son and his bride, sensing that something had happened.

"Okay, you two. What have you discovered?" Ross grinned at his son for the moment, knowing that Rori would speak when he was ready.

"We've talked to Bill and his fellow detectives. We've spoken with Emma. They are not finding any further information on Younge and they should be. Brit and I think that it is someone totally different." Rori hesitated to speak, his eyes searching each of the ones present in the living room before his eyes rested on Brit. She was watching him, cuddled down tight to him. He could see the pain that she was feeling from her beating and sorrowed at that. That shouldn't have happened. Rori wanted the man or woman who was responsible. "We think it's someone different."

"And who would that be?" Richard had reached for a pad of paper and a pen, seeing Silver reaching for her laptop.

"It's a woman." Brit stopped for a moment, not sure how to phrase her words. "And this is who it is." She named the woman, stopping all movement in the room before Richard and Don were nodding.

"You're correct, I think, Brit." Don spoke up. "We've watched her for years, I think since Richard and I were in our teens. There have been vague rumours about her but nothing that could be proven." He sighed as a small grin played around his mouth.

"And it had to be you and Rori God choose to bring her in."

The people gathered in the room stared at Don and then at Brit and Rori before some laughter broke out, relieving the tension. Everyone was aware that God did in fact use His people to bring others to justice.

"So, how do we prove this? And does Emma have the name?" Raleigh reached for her phone, her fingers flying across the keyboard. "She'll get back to us as soon as she can, we all know that."

"She will." Richard was on his feet, heading for the door, having heard a small tap. He frowned as he stared at Abe and Emma. "You two are here? Raleigh just sent you a text with a name."

"I know that she did. I came across it late last night, too late to call anyone. But what happened?" Emma stood for a moment, a frown on her beautiful face. "Which one?"

"Brit. She was beaten today as she headed for her work building." Richard nodded as Abe disappeared, beckoning for Don to come with him. "We've searched around it. The man was arrested. We showed up just as he was walking away, too late to prevent it." He looked around.

"They're both hurting." Emma stood for a moment more, lost in thought. "We get that. Let me talk with them and then we'll talk." She paused at the living room doorway. "Who isn't here?"

Richard grinned as he saw heads turning their way.

"Don's team's wives and the detective. I heard Lily is on her way, just as a friend today. Bill was around this morning at the hospital. We need to end this, Emma, and soon. I fear for Rori and Brit."

Chapter 35

It was late evening before the house was cleared of everyone but Rori and Brit. Rori had simply held Brit as the door closed behind Bevan, the last to leave. Her physical and emotional strengths were spent, he knew. Gathering her into his arms, he walked towards her bedroom and then let her stand on her feet. Kissing her forehead, he walked away, heading for the kitchen to see what needed to be done for the night. Thankfully, everything was neat and tidy.

Rori then moved to Brit's office, staring at the papers on the wall covered in notes and then at the piles of paper tidily stacked on her desk. He sighed. There was a lot of information to digest and he didn't know if they would be able to do it in time. Turning as he heard soft footsteps, Rori moved towards Brit.

"Rori? I am so scared right now." It took a lot for Brit to admit to that and she was showing her vulnerable side to him, something that she never did to anyone.

"I am too, sweetheart." Rori gathered her close once more, turning to find the chair that he preferred in her office and sitting. He reached for the blanket that had been dropped to the floor over the day and covered her. "Here, let me hold you for a while. Do you need anything?"

"No, I don't think so." Brit yawned, pain showing on her face before her head was down on his shoulder and she slept, feeling safe for the moment and also feeling as if she had found her home. That was her last thought before her eyes closed.

Rori opened his mouth to respond and then snapped it closed. He felt the same way. Only he hadn't expected Brit to do what she had, just laying against him. She usually avoided contact with him. His own head went down on hers as he prayed for his lady and before he too slept.

Early the next morning, Rori roused. It was Sunday and that meant church. He sighed to himself, knowing that Brit would not want to attend, not likely, even though they needed to be there. If she didn't go, then Rori would not go either.

Brit rubbed at her eyes, frowning as she realized that she was still in the office. Her head turned slightly as she felt Rori moving before her head went back against him. She felt safe and cherished and didn't want to destroy those feelings by moving from him.

"Rori? It's Sunday. We need to be in church." Brit felt him moving restlessly.

"I know. I just don't know if you want to go, given how your face looks."

"I'll go. I have make up that will cover most of it. I usually don't wear it. Today, I will." Brit moved away from him, intent on starting their coffee and then heading for her bedroom. She didn't feel ready to face the questions and stares but knew that they needed to be there, to hear what Silas had to say that morning.

Rori's head dropped for a moment before he was on his feet and outside, walking the perimeter of the yard and then around the house and garage and then the little shed at the back. Richard and his team had shown him what to look for and recommended that he do his walkabout at least twice a day. He had stared at them and then nodded. Seeing nothing that alarmed him, Rori turned to stare at the house. He didn't know where they would live but he liked this area and home more than his own. That was a discussion for another day.

The next morning, Brit walked away from Rori, heading for her own vehicle. She needed to be at work and so did he. He just didn't want her going on her own. Rori was beginning to hover over her and that she hated. She was used to answering to no one.

Rori walked Brit walk away from him before he was in his own vehicle and following her. He was beside her car door as she stepped out of it, grinning at the frown that she shot his way.

Brit was very nervous, she had to admit. It was hard coming back to where she had been assaulted. She felt Rori's hand on hers as he walked beside her, not saying anything.

"Brit?" Bill's voice calling to her had Brit jumping and then spinning to face him, a hand to her throat. He grinned at the frown he was given. "Let me walk through your building before you go in. I doubt anyone has been inside, but we need to verify that, given what happened to you outside."

Brit's frown deepened even as her hand tightened on her keys. It was her building, after all, and she should be able to walk into it. Only, she couldn't. Something was holding her back. Brit's hand went out as she handed Bill her keys, watching as he and a patrol officer walked to unlock the building.

Bill frowned as he didn't hear any sound from her security system. He pried off the cover and sighed. Someone had gotten to it, disarming it but leaving it looking as if it was still functional. That was not what he wanted to find.

The patrol office returned from his tour of the building, a stern, dark look on his face. He was friends with Brit and had been since their school days.

"Someone has been in here, Bill. And I don't think it was for her good."

"No, it wouldn't be. She's given us a new name to look at." Bill simply looked at Roger as he named someone. "Why that name, Roger?"

"Because she's always had it in for Brit. Her mother was worse. I don't know if Brit was aware of the hatred that they showed towards her. The mother is gone now, but the other lady? She'd be Brit's parents' age if they were still living."

Bill nodded before he turned to the door.

"We'll need to bring in a team, Roger. Go and call it in. I'll speak with Brit and Rori." And that was not something that he was looking forward to.

"Bill? Can I go in? I need to work." Brit tried to move around Bill towards her building, finding him stopping her with a hand to her arm.

"You can't, Brit. Someone has been inside. Your control panel for the security system has been disarmed. We need to search through the building to see what they left. And they will have left something. Tell me what you need and where to find it."

Brit shook her head, not believing that Bill was correct before Rori was pulling her backwards and to her car.

"We'll go to the shop, Brit. Let Bill know what you actually need." Rori frowned. "On second thought, no. Leave everything there. We don't know what might have been tampered with." Rori shoved her into her car and ran around for the driver's seat, speeding away before Brit could react.

Chapter 36

Bill walked into Ross' shop, finding Rebekah at the reception counter. He frowned at her for a moment, not realizing that she worked there part time and he should have.

"Bill? You're here? Ross is on a call but should be done soon. What can you tell us?" Rebekah's voice died as she saw Bill looking around. "You're looking for Rori."

"I am. He and Brit were to be heading this way. He works today, doesn't he?" Bill stopped as he saw Ross approaching them.

"No, Rori was not scheduled for today. He didn't say what his plans were." Ross' arm came around his wife. "What aren't you saying, Bill?"

"Brit's building was got at. Her security system was tampered with. They were to harm her, Rori said. And they're not here." Bill was frustrated, his phone out as he walked away for a moment to make a call, asking for any patrol to search for them". He turned to watch the older couple, seeing the fear that they could no longer hide as they spoke quietly between themselves.

"Bill? What aren't you saying?" Ross waited for Bill to walk back towards them.

"I don't know what to say, Ross. They took off from Brit's building and no one has seen them during the last two hours that I know of." Bill walked away again, this time to call Richard.

"Bill? Where are they?" Richard didn't even wait for Bill to ask any questions.

"We don't know. There was an incident at Brit's building and they left. I thought they would be at his work place but they're not. They're out there somewhere, either on their own or not."

Night fell without anyone finding the couple or hearing from them. They gathered at Ross and Rebekah's home to pray for the couple and that God would be with them, keeping His hand on them. Morning came without any word from either Rori or Brit, sending their families and friends on a new search.

Rori turned from the motel room that they had found the day before, not willing to go to either one's home and be around their families until they made plans. He had finally sent a text an hour before to his father, just letting him know that they were fine and apologizing for being out of touch. That had not been the plan, to not contact the families, but they had lost themselves to their discussions. Those discussions had been somewhat heated at times before Rori had finally just wrapped Brit in his arms and began to pray for her and then for them both.

Brit had snuggled against Rori as he did so, knowing that God was there and would get them through whatever it was and whoever it was that they were facing. They just didn't have to like what they were facing.

Rori had reached for the Bible in the motel room, turning to all the verses that he could find on protection, peace, hope, and whatever suggestion that either one of them had. He could feel the peace that only God gave wafting through his heart and he could see it on Brit's face.

"Rori? Where do we go from here?" Brit hesitated to climb into the car but did so at Rori's urging.

"For now? We head to your home and then to mine. We take what we need from both places for a week or so and then we find somewhere to hide. We contact our families and work with them to solve this. It's getting close to what they call crunch time, sweetheart. I am just so afraid that I will lose you." Rori reached to kiss her before he drove way, searching for anyone following them and not seeing anyone.

"Are we being tailed?" Brit was searching as well. "I need to stop at my building, Rori. There are some things there that I need to take with me." She frowned at him. "You know, there is an apartment above it that is empty. I have never rented it, just maintained it. We could stay there. That way, I could still work and it's close enough to your work that you could work to." Brit was exhausted, her beating still drawing from her strength.

"There is? Okay, so that's what we do." Rori hesitated as he paused at his house before he drove off. "I don't like the feeling that I'm getting there, sweetheart. Someone is waiting there."

Brit nodded as she watched his face. Lord, please protect my fellow. I don't want harm to come to him. Her phone was out as she read through the messages from Becc and Bevan. Please keep my family safe as well as Rori's. Brit simply responded that she was fine and that they had lost track of time discussing what they needed to do.

Brit ran quickly into her house as Rori waited in the car, keeping the engine running. They had no idea who was tracking them but someone was. They had caught a glimpse of a truck following them before Rori had taken a different route. They had no idea how long they would have.

Rori walked through the apartment, nodding to himself. They had stopped to grab enough groceries to get them by for a few days before he had parked in a spot right out in the open. They felt that they were done hiding.

Bill was frustrated with the couple even though he could understand their actions. All the couples finally went on the offensive. Only this time? They had not included anyone in their planning and that had to change. His messages to the couple were very strongly worded.

"Rori? Did you hear from your dad or Richard?" Brit walked into his hug, hugging him back.

"I did. They understand and want to meet with us. Richard suggested tonight, that we come to his place for a meal. I think that would be safe enough, if you're up to it."

Brit nodded before she turned.

"I need to look at what I have to do. Rori? What about your work?"

"It's okay. We're okay that way for now. We sometimes take breaks from it. We need to and this is my time to do that. Show me what you do." Rori followed her down the stairs and into her work room, amazed at how it was laid out. He simply followed her through her day, asking questions when he needed to understand something.

Reaching to set away and lock away what she had been working with, Brit paused, a thought crossing her mind. There was no way that man would be involved, would there? She turned in sudden fear, finding Rori reaching for her. Brit clung to the man trying his best to protect her and provide comfort for her. Sobs shook her body before Rori simply gathered her into his arms and headed up the stairs to the apartment where he found a chair to sit and just hold her.

Chapter 37

A week or more had passed with the investigation being no closer to finishing. That frustrated Rori and Brit who were getting tired of being confined. They had looked at one another that Saturday morning and then rose, intending to put themselves out there with or without their families' support. Little did they know that by doing that their danger had increased to an extreme level.

Walking along the streets of downtown Elmton, Brit stared around them. She could feel the danger moving in on them, just not see it. She felt Rori's hand tightening on hers as he too felt the danger approaching them and not knowing how to avoid it. He tugged her hand to draw her into Ev's diner and then to a private room that they were pointed to.

Ev, Andrew's aunt, approached them, a frown on her face. This was not happening to another one of her young friends, she decided, but knew only too well it was.

"What have you heard, Ev?" Rori simply asked the question that was burning on both his and Brit's lips.

"Not a thing, Rori, and I should. Avery is the same way. Given his law enforcement career, he would hear something from a source and that source is not speaking." Ev was puzzled by the silence.

"So either they don't know, they're terrified, or they're trying to protect us." Rori sat back, staring past

Ev before he looked at her. "How do we do this? I know that Andrew has been speaking with Bill and his team. Silas has been around pray for us. Richard has been following us all over with his team as well as meeting with us. How do we find this person?"

Ev shrugged. She was at a loss, seeing so many of her young friends go through dangerous times.

"I don't know, Rori. I truly do not know what to tell you. Avery would speak with you if he was in today and he's away, out in British Columbia on a holiday." Ev walked away to return with their meals. "Here. Eat and then I'll be back to pray with you."

Rori stared down at his meal, not wanting to eat but knowing that he had to. His thoughts were troubled. He tried to relax, unable to do so for the fear that was running through his heart. He turned to prayer, the only and best thing that he could do at present.

Brit studied her food as well before she reached for her fork. They needed to eat and eat she would. Then, she would corner Ev and talk with her, trying to get a sense of where they should be. She knew that Rori would do the same.

Late that night, Richard raised his head from where he had sat in his office reading. Raleigh had retired, worn out and exhausted not just from her pregnancy but also with worry about her brother. He was on his feet, heading for the back door, a low light in the kitchen showing a friend at the door. Richard opened it to let Murphy and Luke from Abe's team ender.

"You're here late at night, fellows. The coffee's still fresh." Richard watched as the two exchanged a look before looking back at him.

"We are here late. Abe sent us to stay with Rori and Brit. We know where they're living and we like that it is all in one spot. Now, what can you tell us?" Luke spoke for the two of them.

Richard sat the two men down in his office and told them exactly what had been going on, including the fact that Rori and Brit were living in an apartment above her work and that Rori was driving himself back and forth.

The two men from Abe's team shared a look. It was what Emma had told them that they would be doing.

"Any closer to determining who?" Murphy had talked at length with Emma and Abe, the other men of their team involved.

"We have a name that Brit has come up with and it scares me, to tell you the truth. It's a woman who has been here for about a dozen years, watching everyone and yet keeping to herself. Not a lot is known about her. Brit just handed me that name tonight. She's been refusing to before, just because of how afraid she is." Richard handed over a piece of paper with the name scrawled on it.

"Her?" Luke studied the name. They knew it well. She had been back and force between towns, causing trouble but not enough that would get her arrested. This bit this Rori and Brit? It was enough, he decided, and said as much.

"Now we have to come up with a plan to keep those two safe. They won't stay hidden." Murphy knew that only too well. "They've had enough and are wanting to be out and about. Can't say as I blame them. We all grew restless about this time into our adventures."

"We did." Richard had to agree with that. "Now we just have to convince the two that they need us."

"They won't agree, Richard." This came from Luke. He held up his phone. "Rori's been in touch with Abe, asking for his advice. He's worried about you and Raleigh."

"He is and has stated that on many occasions. But we are worried about him. I need to receive the stress on my wife, if at all possible." Richard sighed as a tap came to his door and rose to head for the front door, opening it to find Rori and Brit standing there, Becc and Bevan with them. "What are you four doing here?"

"We need to be, Richard. Becc and Bevan are threatened." Brit was angry. "I want this person. They can't do that to my family and get away with it." Brit almost stomped by him, not even stopping as she saw Murphy and Luke watching her. "You're here? Did Abe or Emma send you? And what can you tell us?"

Murphy and Luke shared a look. Brit was ready to face whoever it was. They just needed some time to plan for that and to get Bill and his team involved. Otherwise, it would be a disaster.

"We need to make some plans, Brit. And we will. Bill needs to be in on the planning or one of his team does. " Luke's hand shoved Brit into a chair, seeing Raleigh hovering in the hallway. "Raleigh? Your experience at this point may well help. Come and talk to her." Luke moved away, finding the men in the hallway, and sending Becc towards her sister.

Chapter 38

Bill stared at Rori the next morning as Rori faced off against him over his desk. He shook his head for a moment before he sighed and then began to pray, begging God to protect his friends.

"You're really going to do that?" Bill had no doubt that he would. His eyes moved to look past Rori, taking in the book shelves and the framed certificates on his office walls.

"We are, Bill. We need to confront that woman. We can't go on with our lives until she is in custody. And we want you to help, you and your team. Either way? We are planning on being out there to force her hand. Luke and Murphy were around last night when we got to Richard's. All three teams are willing to help. And there is another team, Peter's, that will move in to help. We almost have too many people but given how this woman has hidden what she's been doing? We need them."

"I know that you do." Bill sat down into his chair, pointing Rori to one. "We're agreed on this but how do we do it and keep you two safe? You said that she has threatened Becc and Bevan."

"She has. Brit is running scared that she'll lose her family. It's been hard on her raising the two since their parents died. She wouldn't have done it any other way." Rori rubbed at his temple. "And I have begun to remember bits and pieces from when I was first taken captive. I can remember that woman's voice there. And the two Leroys were there. Only they were too drunk to remember what she asked them to do. And that was to dig that hole. I don't know how they did it or if they even did." Rori looked up at that point, seeing Lily had joined them.

Bill hesitated as he looked over his notes. Rori was correct when he stated that the Leroys were there. They were employed by that woman. Only that wasn't common knowledge. A source on the street had come forward to tell Bill that.

"We've moved Becc and Bevan away for now." Rori paced the office, not finding much room to do so. "And yes, they will be safe. They didn't want to leave but left trusting God would keep us safe." He shot a look at Bill and then Lily before he was out of the office and disappearing from the department building.

Lily ran after him but couldn't find him. That frustrated her. The investigation was at a point where they were starting to arrest the lower people in the chain. That would make it much more dangerous for Rori and Brit. She returned to find Bill waiting for her, shrugging as she moved past him. Lily had other investigations that she needed to be about besides this one.

Brit opened the front door to her building, intent on stepping outside for a moment. She felt caged and that she had been inside for too many days. Seeing the woman walking towards her, Brit stepped back inside and quietly and quickly locked the door, moving to stand at a window. Brit opened the blinds just enough that she could peer through.

Hammering at the door and the sounds of someone violently pulling at it had Brit jumping in fear. A hand on her arm had her jumping even more, her own hand up to cover her mouth. Silver stood beside her, a frown on her face.

"Brit?" Silver's voice was barely audible.

"It's her. She's at the door. Why? Who told her?" Brit moved backwards into the room and more towards the back door. "Can we get away?"

"Timothy's out there and will take care of her. For now, we need to stay inside and safe." Silver's hand rested on her weapon even as her phone was out to call Bill. "Bill? We need some help. That woman is out there and trying to get into Brit's building."

Bill dropped the papers that he had in his hand. He had been headed for the copier when Silver called. He ran from the building, calling for help as he did so. Bill was afraid for Brit, that the woman would somehow manage to get inside.

Bill stepped from his car, a puzzled look on his face. Timothy stood near the building, a woman in handcuffs leaning against it. Timothy shook his head at Bill, indicating that they would speak. Officers moved in and removed the woman as Bill approached Timothy.

Timothy pocketed his phone. Brit and Silver were safe and right now? That was the main thing.

"Timothy? Talk to me." Bill waited patiently for Timothy to respond.

"I was patrolling outside and heard all the noise from the front. I found her trying to pry open the steel door." He gave a quick grin. "That didn't work out so well."

"No, I don't imagine that it would. Brit is safe?" Bill was worried about her, hearing Rori's voice approaching him.

"She is. We need to get Rori out of sight too. Silver has Brit in the apartment." Timothy walked around to the back door, unlocking it and shoving Rori inside. Rori ran for the apartment, not waiting for either of the other two men to stop him.

Brit turned as she heard footsteps almost thundering up the stairs and found herself just enveloped in Rori's hug. She clung to him, tears of fear breaking through the strong fence that she had erected.

"You're okay, sweetheart. They've arrested her." Rori couldn't get Brit to look up at him. He sent a puzzled look to Silver who shrugged.

Silver had listened to Brit's words as they had waited for assistance and her heart had fallen. This woman was not the head one, that much was obvious from the muttering that Brit was doing.

"Bill? That woman? She's not the head one. Brit has another name." Silver gave it quietly to Bill, who stared at her in shock and then began to nod. "We need to find that person and do it today. Richard called. There are contracts out on both Brit and Rori. Only no one knows why."

Bill nodded. That name had just come to their attention and Jason was working through the investigation involving it.

"I know, Silver. I know. But they're not going to stay hidden any longer. I can't fault them for that." Bill watched Rori as he turned Brit to the stairs and walked down them. "They're going to be out there, Silver. How do we manage that? They're newlyweds, no matter how it happened, and need to be out there doing what newlyweds do."

"I know, Bill. We've been through stuff, all of us." Silver paced before she turned to Bill. "I have an idea that I need to run by Richard and then we'll talk." Silver was away, finding Rori and Brit waiting for her. She shoved them out of the back door and towards Timothy who simply opened his truck doors for them to hop in before he drove away, heading for Richard's home.

Chapter 39

Turning as he heard soft footsteps, Rori reached for Brit. They had simply come home to Rori's place, praying that they would be safe. Rori had shaken his head at Richard when Richard had questioned him, asking that Richard pull his team from them. They all needed that break. Instead, Rori asked for prayer as he and Brit had some decision to make.

Brit clung to Rori before he turned them to find seats on the couch. He kept Brit wrapped tight in his arms, praying aloud for them both and for the investigators.

"It's getting close to being done, sweetheart." Rori's voice was low. "How do we stay safe?"

"We can't, Rori, not on our own. God has to be there and He is. He has been protecting us all along. He has sheltered us under His wings and kept us hidden under His hand in the hollow of the rock. We just need to trust Him. I don't want to lose you or lose any of our families."

"And that is a real worry. The man who is in charge is vicious. More and more people are approaching Richard and his team, telling them what has transpired over the years. Richard is feeding all that to Bill and his team." Rori paused. "How do we draw him out, though, without one of us being hurt?"

"I know. How do we do it?" Brit grew quiet, almost asleep.

Rori studied her beloved face before he sighed. They needed to sleep. Only now was not a good time for that. He too slept, feeling safe in his home for once. He didn't sense that someone after them was outside their home. Neither one knew that Richard had called in Don and that Don's men were outside, protecting them.

Early morning found the couple on their feet, staring at one another before they both nodded. They had talked as they awoke and had come up with a plan. They just weren't sure how well it would work or if they would survive.

Locking the door behind them, Rori headed for his truck, Brit keeping step with him. They were heading out for breakfast before they headed in for work. Today, Brit would be working from Ross' shop, her laptop firmly in her grasp as she climbed into the vehicle. Rori nodded as he saw trucks pulling out around them. Someone was there, watching out for them. He frowned as he saw a car trying to pull in front of them to stop them. This was where it got dangerous.

Rori watched the car pull out and follow them. He sighed. He just couldn't catch a break with his bride, not even to take her out for breakfast. Parking at Ev's diner, Rori reached for Brit's hand, a prayer whispering in the truck before he reached to kiss her. They had both decided that they were not hiding any more, sensing that it, whatever it was, was coming to a head and to a head quickly. They had spent the night in prayer and then just waiting before God, rising with the confidence that He was in control and would protect them. They just didn't know how He would do that or if one of them would graduate to heaven in the next few days.

Ross turned from where he had been studying a new diagram for a new product and watched the couple. Yes, he decided, they are a couple at last. Everyone could see that but he knew that Brit had to fight through that battle with God on her own. They had been praying for her. He sighed as he looked at Rori. Things could go badly very quickly, he decided, but knew that he could not step in and solve anything for his son, not as he could when Rori was a young child. Ross and Rebekah could only stand beside their son and his bride and help to pick up the pieces when it was over. He knew full well that Rori would never be the same. Raleigh hadn't and that had saddened her parents.

Settling down in an empty office, Brit opened her laptop, preparatory to working. She could hear the faint conversation and laughter coming from the work floor and smiled. Rori was happy and content here, she decided. She frowned as a thought crossed her mind and was on her feet, hunting for Ross.

"Ross? Do you have a moment?" Brit stood beside him as he watched his crew working.

"For you, Brit? Always. You look worried." Ross pointed back towards where she was set up for the day.

"I am." Brit sat back in the chair, her eyes on her father-in-law, a man who she was beginning to love as her own father. She sorely needed a father's counsel right then. "We have never been able to figure out why this has happened or who was behind it. We have come up with names and those people have been arrested." Brit bit at her lip, not sure how to continue.

"And you have a thought as to why." Ross nodded at Bill who stood just outside the door, causing Bill to not enter.

"I do. What if it's not me or not Rori? What if it's you or Rebekah? Who would take over your shop if you had to close it?"

Ross nodded. Brit had gone right to the centre of what he and Rebekah had discussed the night before as they met with Andrew and his wife, Phoebe. They had come to that consensus, that the younger couple was not the target as much as it had seemed.

"We were discussing that last night with Andrew and Phoebe. I think that you are correct, Brit. If the shop closes, no one takes it on. Each piece of glass work is unique to each shop. I mean, they can try to copy it but it's not the same. We have a unique spot in our trade and crafts. I've been doing this since Dad set up the business. Rori is the third one of our family to carry it on. We have expanded over the years in what we offer and those wares are sold all over the world through our online store. Each piece is not the same as another one just because that's how it is. The men and women who work here? They have been here for years. They are training new staff but we keep our workforce small. Doe that answer your question?"

"I think it does. If someone forced you to close down, then they would take over your suppliers and customers?" Brit was struggling to understand how this all worked. "With my work, they would just go to someone else." Brit was highly respected in her work even though she was younger than most of the gemologists that she knew.

"They might but customers are picky. They know what they like and want. Someone else might not fit what they are looking for but some would go to a rival." Ross sighed, knowing just who it might be. "And I think I know who it is. Bill?"

Brit jumped as she sensed someone else in the room and stared wide-eyed at Bill.

"Bill?" Her voice was low and fragile, her emotions raw and open in that voice.

"I think that you are correct, Brit. That's what we're hearing now that we have made some arrests. It's not you or Rori except to get to Ross. I have that name, Ross. It actually came up this morning and that's why I'm here, to discuss it with you." Bill turned and walked away, not seeing Rori watching him before he looked towards the offices.

Rori walked away that afternoon from his work, Brit's hand tight in his. Both of them had spent time with Ross, just praying and then making plans. Those plans now included both Ross and Rebekah, who had refused to be left out. The young couple were worried about the older couple but had to agree. The only way to solve this was for both couples to work on drawing out whoever it was.

Chapter 40

Ross started to turn as he stood in his backyard that evening before he felt the end of a revolver jammed into his side. He sighed. That man, as Brit termed it, had found him. Now to activate their plan and keep all of them alive. The other three were in the house as he was forced that way. Ross knew that the man whom they suspected would be on his own. It was how he worked and had all of his life.

Forced to walk towards his house, Ross tried his best to come up with a way to escape and could think of nothing. Rebekah was away with Raleigh at a church meeting. Rori and Brit had been there but had left as well. He had no idea if they were safe or not. He could only pray that God had them hidden somewhere safe.

"In the house." Ross heard the guttural command from behind him but didn't feel the weapon any more. Come to think of it, he decided, it had not been a gun. He swung around, his fist back before he landed it with a hard crunch on the man's jaw. That man crumped to the ground and didn't move. Ross reached for his phone, calling for help, before he locked himself into the house, text messages out to both Rebekah and Rori not to come around. He had just had an incident and needed them to stay safe.

Rori reached for Brit, hearing her cry of dismay as she read the text message. He wrapped her close, his eyes closing as he prayed for his father and begged God to keep him safe.

"Rori? Who?" Brit shoved away from him and began to pace his living room. They had gone back to his home that night, not sure which home to live in.

"I don't know but I suspect it was the man we were after. Bill has that name and said that he would reach out again to us when he had more information." Rori's hands waved in the air. "I know. I know. That's no comfort. I get that." Rori was angry, not at Brit or Bill but at the situation that they found themselves still in.

Brit stalked away from him, heading for the door. She stopped before she reached it, suddenly not able to go any further. Rori had followed her, puzzled that she stopped suddenly.

"Brit? The door?" Rori made a move to go around her but stopped as her hand reached out to grab his arm. "We're not answering the door?"

"No, we're not. Someone who means us harm is out there. Where can we hide?" Brit jumped as a hand hammered at the door.

Rori looked around before he grabbed Brit's hand and tugged her with him.

"In here." He shoved her into the spare room and then felt along a section of the wall. The wall swept open and Rori shoved Brit inside before he followed her and then swung the wall closed once more. He couldn't see her face but he felt how hard she was holding on to him.

The couple could hear the slamming open of their front door and then the heavy footsteps as two men tromped through the house, seeking to find them. Brit hid her face against her groom, not wanting to know what was transpiring outside, even though they did need to know.

An hour later, Rori's phone chimed with a text message. He squinted at it as he heard Brit softly reading it. It was safe for them to come out but neither made a move to do so. Brit simply claimed Rori's phone and asked for proof that the person sending the message really was who he said he was.

Bill stared at his phone for a moment, disbelief on his face before he shook his head and showed the text to Lily, who grinned as well. He took a picture of himself standing in their living room and sent it on. Neither he or Lily heard anything until soft footsteps alerted them to the fact that they were not alone. They turned to find Rori and Brit standing in the doorway to the bedroom wing, watching them.

"Where were you two?" Bill bit back more words, knowing that he couldn't say them.

"We found somewhere safe to hide and no, I won't say where. Did you arrest the men?" Rori was standing up as straight as he could muster, ready to argue with Bill or Lily if that happened.

"We did. And we have arrested the man you named. He tried to take on your father on his own. That didn't work out so well." Bill grinned for a moment as Rori laughed.

"No, it wouldn't. Dad may be older but his work has built up his muscles. Besides, he was ready for a fight of some kind." Rori's body sagged for a moment. "Is it over, Bill? Can we relax now?"

"For tonight, I would like to see you and your families under one roof. Richard's would be a good spot for that. And yes, he is outside with part of his team, the other two with your parents and Raleigh. They are taking no chances. And I hear tell that Don is moving in as well." Bill waved as he walked away, a grin on his face at Brit's loud and furious protest.

Rori shrugged as Brit spun, her mouth open to complain before she snapped it closed. He simply swept her into a hug before heading for the bedroom and their duffle bags. They hadn't unpacked yet, not sure if they would be staying there or not. Obviously, they wouldn't be.

Brit stared at Richard as he stood in the entry way, a mutinous look on her face. He simply grinned at her and reached for the bag in her hand, waiting for them to exit the house, the security system set and the door locked. She stared back at it before she was running for Bill, a hand out to stop him.

"Bill? They didn't break in the door. They had a key. The door was locked." Brit wrapped her arms around herself, still deeply afraid.

"That what they said. And we know where the key came from. You're safe, Brit. Trust me on that." Bill watched with compassion as her face crumpled for a moment as she struggled with her emotions and the tears that she refused to let fall before she was walking away, a hand out for Rori's.

Rori simply walked away with his bride, heading for Richard and Raleigh, knowing that the end was in sight for them. Fatigue was hitting both he and Brit hard and that was to be expected. He had seen it in the others.

Chapter 41

Four days later, Rori simply sat on a loveseat at Richard's home and swept Brit into a hard hug. Their ordeal was finally over. Bill, Lily, and Jason had all appeared to share the celebratory lunch that the ladies had prepared. Silas and Madigan, their pastoral couple, had shown up as well, simply grinning as Rori grinned at them. Their story had been shared with Brit who had been shocked as she remembered the body found in their church. She had not realized the ramifications of that find.

Bill watched all of the family members, seeing the relief and happiness that they were showing. Conversation had been light and laughter prominent during the meal that they has shared and then the time of prayer had been filled with praise. He looked down at his notes before he raised his head once more.

"Okay, people. Here what we know. Rori? Brit? It really wasn't all about your occupations or what you made. It went back years to even before your father took over the business. Someone wanted to take over your grandfather's life and reputation, thinking that they would be wealthy. This person didn't realize that it took hard work and contacts for your father to build what he has today. And you have continued that as well. Brit, you were incidental to this all. Somehow, someone saw you and Rori together at a church meal and decided that you were a couple. They then decided to force you two to marry.

"Rori? You were kidnapped to try and force this. You apparently had refused and were deprived of food and water and sleep. And yes, the Leroys were the ones who dropped you into that pit. They were too drunk to remember doing that. They are facing many charges themselves. And whoever was behind it was behind everything that happened to you both." Bill stopped speaking for a moment.

"Who was it, Bill?" Rori just had to ask the question that everyone wanted an answer to.

"Who was it? It wasn't someone who was obvious. The ones who had approached you? They're the ones who were drawn in to the scheme by promises of wealth, promises that the culprit had no intention of keeping." Bill paused to take a drink from his bottle of water, his eyes on Ross. His next words would bring a sort of devastation and sadness to his friend.

Ross was watching Rori closely and then watched his daughter. He could tell that the news would not be good and that worried him. He had an idea as to who it was and had discussed that with Rebekah. She had simply agreed that he was likely correct in his guess. Then, they had bowed their heads to pray for their son and his bride as well as for their daughter and her husband. This news, if they were correct, would be hard to digest.

Bill sighed. This was part of his investigations that was always the hardest, sharing with the families who had been behind their problems.

"Who was it?" Bill still hesitated, sharing a look with Jason and Lily. "It was your cousin, Douglas

Reade, Ross. He is the one who wanted it all without working for it. He really doesn't have much money and his reputation is in tatters. He has always been one who lived big in public but was a miser in his personal life. That is why he never married. Douglas has stated that he resented the fact that you had something that you could take over and grow to what it is today. He was envious of your family life, not having that. His parents didn't like him and treated him wrong in private but portrayed loving parents in public. This warped his mind and his thinking to the point that he wanted revenge on you and your family when he couldn't get what you had. I'm sorry that it took us so long to find this out. And we're sorry, Rori and Brit, that you had to go through what you did."

Bill, Lily, and Jason walked away about an hour later, tiredness dragging at their feet. Another investigation involving friends had been completed, not necessarily the way that they would have wished but it was as God had planned. They had to remember that.

Epilogue

Six months later, Rori was on a search for his bride as he still called her. She wasn't at her work. She wasn't at his work. And he couldn't find her in the new house that they had decided to buy, selling their own to combine their household. He stood for a moment before he grinned and headed for the outdoors. Brit had set up an office in a shed that she had converted at the back of their property, not to do her actual work but as a retreat for them both.

Brit looked up as she sensed someone near her, not afraid this time that it was someone ready to harm her. Instead, she was on her feet, enveloped in the hug that her groom was offering her. Her head rested against Rori's chest, hearing his heart beat and knowing that her love for him was just growing day by day as was his for her.

"I couldn't find you, sweetheart. Have you been out here long?" Rori didn't release her, content to hold her.

"For a couple of hours. Just returning some emails and whatnot. I'm sorry I was hiding on you." Brit simply grinned up at him. "Bill called."

"He did? And?" Rori just waited for her to speak, knowing that she would when she was ready.

"He did. Everyone has taken a plea deal, even Douglas. There was just too much evidence against him." Brit was glad for that. She had dreaded facing any of them in court.

"They did? God did answer our prayers, sweetheart. He is good to us and protected us in so many ways." Rori stared down at her, praise rising in his heart that she was his. "We may never have married if this had not happened. I don't like what we went through, but it did bring us together. Now that all of this is behind us, we can move forward. I have a cabin out in the woods rented for the next week. I was hoping to persuade my bride to run away with me."

"You were, were you?" Brit didn't answer right away, causing concern in Rori. "We need that, Rori. We truly do. And we need to do something for our families. They went through so much with us and with all of Richard's team going through what they did."

"And we will. Richard has already reached out that way. He and Raleigh want to host something, now that their little one is here."

Brit nodded, a sober thought crossing her mind. Would she and Rori ever be parents? And if they were, what kind of parents would they be?

"Have I told you today that I love you?" Rori reached to kiss her.

"You have. I love you too, my love." Brit turned from his arms, gathering up her work, and then waiting as he closed and locked the door behind him.

Rori reached for her stuff as she called it and then for her hand. Life was good at the present time, finally settling into somewhat normalcy. But that normalcy was not what it would have been a year ago. The adventure that they had shared had changed that but God had led them, had walked the path before them, and was leading them forward to be the hands and feet on earth for Him.

Dear Readers

Thank you for picking up the story of Rori and his love, Brit. It has taken a while to write. Neither one was forthcoming with their story. And I am still healing from a shoulder fracture in April of this year with major surgery to repair it, which has impacted my writing.

God was there all the way through their adventure. Even when He seemed to be silent, He was there. He never leaves us or forsakes us no matter what we face. He is in control and does shelter us when we need that.

Bill, Lily, Andrew, Silas, Richard and his team, and Richard's brother, Riley, all had adventures as they call them as did Abe and Emma and their team. My characters can't stay out of another's story, walking back and forth freely. I like that. It keeps the stories flowing as they add to the mixture. Bill's story is *Hidden in the Hollow.* Lily's is *Lily.* Andrew's is *The Potter's Hands.* Richard and his team: *Timothy, Silver, Stephen, Naomi,* and *Richard.* Riley's is *Riley.* Abe and Emma and their team's stories are in *His Guardians.* Silas and Madian's is *Strong Courage.* Jason didn't have a story but his sister, Julia and her husband, Mark's are in *His Warriors.*

May God richly bless you as you walk forward in your life, your eyes on Him. There are times when it seems dark and lonely but you are never ever alone. God has promised that.

Ronna

Milton Keynes UK
Ingram Content Group UK Ltd.
UKHW022135291124
451915UK00011B/695